For Brittany, Kasey, and Lana.
I'm forever thankful we met. 🖤

THE MAD LOVE SERIES

Sunshine

AND

MADNESS

Cover Design | Book Design and Typesetting: Green Spark Publishing
Conceptual Editor: Kasey LeAlma
Line Editor: Lana Staux
Copy Editor: Natalia Leigh, Enchanted Ink Publishing
Proofreader: Brittany Riley

ISBN: 978-1-963126-09-9 (E-book)
ISBN: 978-1-963126-06-8 (Paperback)
ISBN: 978-1-963126-11-2 (Hardback)

Second Edition: February 2025
Published by Green Spark Publishing
Thank you for the support of the author's rights.

Printed in the United States of America

Sunshine

AND

MADNESS

I HARDLY REMEMBERED ANYTHING FROM THE NIGHT before. Sometimes I wished New York would sleep once in a while.

Fuck, I hope I did okay last night. God, I wanted the hammering in my head to stop. *Shit, this is getting old.*

I peeled my eyes open and saw nothing but a white blur for a long moment. Blinding death rays of sunlight flashed into the room. Someone had opened the fucking curtains. Vision still blurry, I made out the familiar silhouette next to the large window of my master bedroom. Honking cars and sirens filled my ears as I lay on my stomach, groaning like a starved zombie.

I'd swear off women if I didn't like pussy so much. The last thing I remembered was hitting on some blond chick in the bar area of the Hard Rock Cafe before some dick—probably her boyfriend—sucker punched me. I woke up in a jail cell at three in the fucking morning. I had no idea how I got home. Even though it was my first run-in in years, my manager was going to be pissed.

"Wake up, asshole." It was the deep—and obviously unhappy—voice of Ethan Miller. "Do you know how much of a fucking headache you've caused me?" He moved away from the window, his blue-gray eyes boring into me as he ran a hand through his short dark hair. He walked into my master bathroom after tossing his navy blazer onto the bed.

I sat up, trying to hide my face from the light. "No, but I'm guessing you're gonna tell me."

He came back and shoved a glass of water into my hand. Some drops sloshed onto my dark boxers.

Son of a bitch, that's cold.

"You're lucky I'm not only your band manager, but also your best friend. Because I don't know any other managers who would put up with your shit." Ethan dropped two painkillers into my palm. "I swear, you're the only member of the band who gives me problems." He straightened his fitted black tee. His pale features expressed just how displeased he was with me.

I swallowed the pills and downed the water. "Do me a favor? Stop yelling." I stood and made my way to the bathroom to wash up. Unfortunately, Ethan followed.

"Do you have any idea how many fans you disappointed last night?" Ethan leaned against the doorpost of my bathroom while I splashed tap water onto my face from the chrome faucet. "Do you even care?"

I glanced at him in the full-wall mirror before drying my face off. "What do you want me to say, Ethan?"

His eyes narrowed. "You know what? Fine. This is *your* career."

He started to walk away, but I trailed behind him with a bemused grin. Couldn't help it. He'd always cared more about my music career than I did.

"Look, I'm sorry. Just give me a couple hours to shake this fucking hangover, then we can deal with this shit," I said as he grabbed his blazer and headed to the private elevator door of my penthouse.

His features relaxed as he let out a breath. "Fine." He turned and strode through the mud room and hallway, into my large living area, which had a beautiful panoramic view of NYC's high-rises. "I talked to the video producer today about the situation. He's giving you *one* more chance. His exact words were, 'Stay out of the public eye, and we'll be good.' So, you'd better get your shit straight."

Totally forgot about that fucking music video. When did my music career become so . . . out of my control? Hell, I couldn't even date who I wanted to without consulting my publicist.

I rolled the tension from my shoulders. "I didn't even write that fucking ballad." I plopped onto my plush sectional, which hugged the wall across from the ridiculously huge TV.

"If you're thinking about sabotaging the music video shoot too, please warn me."

"Fuck you." I let out a breath. "Do you think I planned on getting into a fight last night just so I didn't have to perform? That's a little extreme, Ethan. Don't you think?"

With a shrug, he asked, "I don't know. Is it? What do you want, Lucas?"

My brow furrowed. "What're you talking about?"

"For the past year, you've been wandering aimlessly through your career. No Blood, No Alibi's record contract expires soon. Where are you gonna go from there?"

"I don't know, man. I don't know." I glanced down at my hands. What was I supposed to say? That I'd lost my passion for music? That I'd somehow lost my way on this road to fame? That I felt empty inside? I couldn't fucking tell him any of that. He'd never understand.

"When do we start shooting?" I grabbed the remote off the glass coffee table and flipped through the channels before landing on an old NHL game. I'd always wanted to play hockey, but music was all I could handle in high school.

"The producer just needs to find the love interest, then they'll be ready." Ethan stared at the TV, paying more attention to the game than to me. Good. He glanced at me. "We need to do something for your fans to make up for last night's shit show."

Did he think that wasn't lingering in the back of my mind? I already knew I had to make things right with them. I didn't even know why I'd gotten so drunk. Hell, I didn't know the fucking guy I'd fought. How had I let things go so far?

I'm a goddamn rock star. So, why didn't I feel like one?

I ARRIVED AT THE BALLET STUDIO A FEW MINUTES EARLY and did some stretching to warm up my muscles for the long day of teaching. I lengthened my stiff hamstrings on the cold floor in front of the mirrored wall; after my recovery, it was a must.

I'd kept the old cherry blossom wallpaper from the Japanese restaurant my ballet studio used to be. It matched the half-sleeve tattoo on my right forearm. The theme suited me. For now, the cheap white linoleum tiles were good enough until I could save money for a remodel. I'd added a brass barre to the mirror-lined wall for my students.

The metal-framed glass door swung open, and my best friend, Mia, strode in. Her dark almond-shaped eyes had a glint of sadness in them. She was a beautiful woman with high cheekbones, a sharp jawline, and an adorably small yet proportionate nose. She tossed her black tote onto the smooth worn surface of the mahogany reception desk that stood near the entrance. Her outfit screamed springtime; she wore a light blue blouse, jeans, and black flats. Her gaze met mine in the large mirror.

"Wake up on the wrong side of the bed?" I asked her as I spread my legs into the splits and leaned forward onto my forearms. Luckily, my body was still limber, though I had gained a bit of weight in my lower body, which I was completely fine with. Eating could've been my part-time job. I loved food, especially steak. Mia had accused me of being a zombie in a past life. I didn't disagree.

Mia continued to stare at me for another second or two, as if thinking about telling me what was on her mind. "I broke up with Don."

"What? Why?" I stood, and my black wrap skirt swished as I walked up to her.

"He told me he wanted me to quit my job after we get married," Mia said, walking around to the back of the receptionist's desk.

Not only was she my best friend, but Mia also worked for me as my personal assistant and substitute teacher. We'd been in the same dance company together, but when her mother passed away about the same time I was injured, she quit dancing altogether. I knew she missed it, but she wasn't ready to take the stage yet.

"I'm so sorry." I pulled her into a hug. "I didn't know you two were talking about marriage."

She murmured into my shoulder, "We weren't. I was content with the way things were, but he wanted more, and I just couldn't be what he wanted. Not now, anyway."

"You know what we should do? We should go see my dad's band tonight. I think they're playing at a bar in Newark." I pulled away from her. Sure, he'd missed dinner last night, but his band was good. "We can have a few drinks and headbang the night away." I giggled.

Mia did too, her brown eyes brimming with tears. Oh yeah, she definitely needed this.

"That sounds great, Jules," she said.

"Good. Now that we have that settled, there's another issue." I went back to the floor and continued to stretch.

She rummaged through some receipts on the desk. "Is it about the theater rent for the spring recital?"

I nodded and climbed to my feet. "I don't think we'll sell enough tickets to pay for it. We can always do a fundraiser, but there's no guarantee there either."

"So, what're we gonna do?" She set the papers down and pulled her long brown hair into a messy bun.

"I'm going to get a second job. Part-time only." I placed one leg on the barre and began to relevé on the other foot.

Mia's face scrunched as she asked, "How're you gonna find the time? We barely have any as it is."

I let out a breath. "I know. I need to find something that's short-term or seasonal, working only a few hours a night."

"Bartending?" she suggested, lifting her slim shoulder.

"I tried that and failed miserably, if you recall." I rolled my eyes. "I haven't mixed a drink since."

Mia laughed. "So, what then? You're limited on the type of jobs you can do at night."

"I know. I need to find something though," I said, switching legs on the barre.

"You could always be a stripper. They make good money." She grinned and waggled her brow.

I shot her a narrow-eyed glare. I didn't have anything against the occupation, but I couldn't see that for myself. Given the shape I was in, I wasn't sure I could even pull off pole dancing; I was still strong, just not *that* strong. "You're hilarious."

"What? I'd stop by and toss a few ones your way," she teased.

"Oh, is that all I'm worth?" A grin crept onto my face.

"Sorry, my boss doesn't pay me enough." She rummaged through her purse and pulled out a stick of cherry-flavored ChapStick. "Anyway, what happened to that guy you were talking to?"

I took my leg off the barre, straightening my black wrap skirt over my matching short-sleeve leotard. "Which guy?" I knew who she was talking about.

"Shawn?" She cocked a brow at me.

With a shrug, I said, "Nothing. He stopped calling me."

"He stopped calling, or you stopped answering?"

"What difference does it make?" I smirked.

She huffed. "I liked him. He seemed like a pretty stable guy."

Sure, Shawn was a lawyer and a damn good one at that. He had his own place and a nice car. But I couldn't see myself moving forward with him, plus the sex sucked. And I could never be with someone who couldn't make me come.

"Why don't you date him, then?" I snipped. I hadn't meant for it to come out so bitchy, but she caught it.

"One of these days, you're gonna have to get over your shit. Not everyone is gonna leave you." She placed her hands on her hips.

My brows came together. "I don't know what you're talking about." I made my way into the back office and slammed the door. We were pretty much used to each other's shit talk, but sometimes she just got on my nerves.

I HELD GROUP CLASSES FROM MORNINGS TO EVENINGS and fit in private lessons wherever I could. Sometimes I would go a little over time simply because I loved working with my students. They were amazing and full of so much potential, even though sometimes they drove me up the wall.

Damn, this day flew by.

After I locked the door to the studio, Mia and I sanitized everything and straightened up the studio before we grabbed our bags and headed out the door.

"You think I can raid your closet tonight?" she asked as we made our way to my apartment building a couple blocks away.

I nodded. "Like I can stop you."

Mia really had become like a sister to me throughout the years. She'd stayed with me for six months as I recovered from my dance injury. I was so thankful to have her in my life.

We kept a slow steady pace and finally arrived at the brick residence, then ambled through the small lobby and climbed the stairs to my apartment. We took turns in the shower before choosing our outfits.

I didn't dress up or anything, just wore my usual dark blue skinny jeans, Doc Martens, and a loose cropped black tee. Mia, on the other hand, stuck out like a sore thumb in a flowery top I'd hidden in the back of my closet. The miniskirt she wore showcased her powerful tanned dancer's legs, and, of course, she wore red four-inch heels. Our styles when it came to fashion were extremely different; some people asked why we were even friends.

On the way to the bar, I texted my dad, telling him we'd be there. As expected, he didn't respond. He was probably setting up or busy flirting with the groupies. Couldn't blame him for living it up. God knew he hadn't been able to do that when I was younger and dependent on him.

The taxi dropped us off in the dirt parking lot of a wood-paneled building otherwise known as Stuckies. This *would* be the type of bar my dad's band would perform in.

It sounded like the band had begun their first set as we were ID'd by the bouncer at the entrance. We walked in to In Your Head performing a cover of "Paralyzer" by Finger Eleven. It was released in the early 2000s but still rocked, especially given the way my dad played the drums. It almost sounded more metal than anything.

Mia pointed to the younger-looking guy playing the

guitar on the small wooden stage. "Is that the new guitarist?" Her eyes widened as we walked over to a high-top table.

I yelled, "Yeah, his name is Cameron. I think he used to sub for Maroon 5."

She nodded.

"Come on." I grabbed her hand and pulled her out onto the crowded dance floor. We gyrated and jumped to the beat of the music. I waved at my dark-haired dad, who sat behind the drum set, rocking the hell out of the song. That was one thing we had in common: a passion for music.

God, I loved losing myself in the rhythm. I didn't have to worry about form or stage cues when it was just me and the melody. My body moved with Mia's among the chaos of the crowd. We smiled at each other as the song ended.

"I'm going to get us some drinks," I told her before walking in the bar's direction. The small building was so full that I had to force my way through the crowd.

Cold liquid splashed onto me, soaking my T-shirt. I gasped, holding up my arms in shock at the impact.

"What the fuck?" I exclaimed as the band started playing their next song. It sounded like an original, but I didn't fucking care at that point.

The guy stood there with his dark hoodie. And why the fuck was he wearing shades? He continued to stand there with his now-empty glass in hand. The girl he'd been talking to appeared to be holding back her laughter. I had half a mind to punch her and the clueless guy in the fucking face.

"Um, are you just gonna act like that didn't happen?" I

stood there with my arms crossed, probably looking like a drowned rat.

Finally, the guy faced me. What was with the hoodie? *Fucking weirdo.*

"Obviously, it was an accident." The scent of liquor filled my nose as he leaned close, voice deep and raspy. Despite my black combat boots, he still stood about half a foot taller than me.

"That's not quite an apology, dude," I retorted, eyes narrowing.

"I don't see the need for one," he replied. A corner of his mouth rose, which set my blood on fire in the worst way possible.

My nostrils flared. "Oh, so that drink magically ended up on me all by itself?" I placed a hand on my hip.

He furrowed his brow, apparently annoyed with me. "It was an accident. Maybe you should watch where you're going, Sunshine."

Oh, hell no. I was going to kick this guy's ass. "Fuck you, asshole. You owe me an apology," I yelled, jabbing my index finger into his rock-hard chest. The girl he'd been talking to excused herself.

He faced me with a smug grin. "You're kind of feisty."

My cheeks warmed, and definitely not in a good way. "And you're kind of a douche." I pushed up onto my tippy-toes, getting close enough to make out the sharp lines of his jaw and full lips. *Kissable lips.* This guy looked familiar. My heart rate had gone through the roof. Who did this guy think he was, anyway?

"Uh, Jules? I thought you were getting drinks." Mia walked up to us. A dark-haired, blue-eyed man stood beside her. Who the hell was that?

I let out a breath. "Jackass!" I walked away from the whole thing before I did something that would get me arrested. Pushing through the crowd, I was in desperate need for air.

Heart still pounding in my ears, I burst through the back door of the building, and the crisp spring breeze hit my cheeks. I placed my hands on my knees and leaned over, trying to recover from the adrenaline rush.

"Fucking asshole," I whispered, glancing back at the open metal door. The pulse in my neck still thrummed as I continued to breathe in and out. *In and out.*

Mia walked out shortly after. "Are you okay?" she asked, placing a hand on my back. "The only other time I've seen you angry like that was when Christy Herring threatened to beat me up after dance practice."

Mia always knew how to calm me down. I cracked a grin. "It got her off your back, didn't it?" My breathing had gone back to normal. The cold air had helped. There was no way I would go back in if he was still there.

She smiled and nodded. "Well, you don't have to worry about that guy anymore. He left," Mia said as I straightened, taking another cleansing breath.

Thank God.

"The band is taking a break if you want to go say hi to your dad," she added.

Might as well. Maybe it'll get my mind off that asshole.

"I just need to go to the bathroom." I grimaced at the Rum scent. My preferred beverage was Crown and Coke.

After I attempted to dry the remnants of spilled alcohol from my shirt, Mia and I walked up to the band, who had a table next to the stage. It looked like they were sharing a few pitchers of beer.

My middle-aged dad, Rick Blackwell, walked up and embraced me. He and I had the same chestnut eyes, and his short peppered beard complemented his spiky brown hair. "I'm so glad you came out, Jay Bird. And sorry about dinner the other night. I'll make it up to you."

Like I hadn't heard that before.

I let out an exasperated breath at the sound of my nickname. But he'd called me that ever since I could remember, so I let it go. "Yeah, Mia had to get out tonight," I said.

He glanced at Mia and gave her a hug as well. "Come on, sit down. We have about fifteen minutes before our second set."

Mia and I sat at the circular table.

"Hey, Gale," I said to the lead guitarist.

The bleach-blond woman wore a torn black crop top, showing off a belly button ring, distressed black jeans, and Converse. I was sixteen when she joined the band, and I'd always looked up to her. She pushed me to do things that were out of my comfort zone, like opening my own dance studio.

"You guys sound really good, as usual," I said as the jukebox blended with the conversations of the patrons.

"Thanks, babe." She leaned over and gave me a side hug. "I haven't seen you at one of these in a while. Been busy?"

I nodded. "Yeah, the business has been taking all my time these days."

Gale crossed her arms on the table. "Well, I'm glad you made some time to come out and play tonight."

"Actually, I'm really here for Mia." I glanced over at my best friend, who'd sparked up a conversation with the new guitarist. His hair was longer on top and tapered on the sides, and his green eyes were captivating.

"Do me a favor and don't forget about yourself," Gale said, interrupting me practically gawking at Cameron.

What? I could acknowledge a beautiful human being.

"You know me. I'm all about self-care." I really wasn't. I didn't even know the last time I'd had a manicure.

She shot me a glare. "I *do* know you, Jules, which is why I'm telling you."

"Hey, don't worry. I'm here now, having a blast." My lips curved up.

"Five minutes," the long-haired bass player, Carter, said after he'd chugged his glass of beer.

All the guy band members took the stage within seconds of his announcement. Before Gale stood and followed suit, she said, "Don't let another six months pass before coming to see us again."

I rolled my eyes. "No promises."

She flipped me the bird as she walked up the steps to the stage. I just laughed. That was Gale.

Part of me would always have a crush on her. How had

my dad been in a band with her for so long without hitting on her? She had a beautiful strong jawline, dark eyes, and full lips. If she'd wanted to, she probably could've become a model. Maybe that was why Dad never did anything. She was *way* out of his league.

We spent the rest of the night taking shots, only to dance all the alcohol out of our systems. From the sweat glistening on her forehead to the huge smile on her face, I could tell Mia was having a good time, whether she wanted to admit it or not. At one point, we stopped dancing to watch Gale shredding on the guitar. That woman was fucking epic.

Mia and I called for a cab about midnight. We ended up crashing on my loveseat and watching *Gossip Girl*.

In the back of my mind, the thought of that asshole still lingered like an annoying fucking itch.

THAT GIRL WAS CRAZY. WHAT KIND OF APOLOGY DID SHE want? She was the one who ran into me.

Ethan dropped me off at my penthouse after the incident. We didn't need another publicity issue on our hands. For some reason, that girl's fiery eyes had caused sparks in my mind when they'd narrowed. How she'd pursed her lips, nostrils flaring because of me.

What the hell? I snapped back to reality. That girl was probably fucking trouble. Not that I was any better, but still. I was good with my one-night stands. *No emotional connections. Just keep it physical.* Thank God I wouldn't *ever* have to see her again.

Ethan woke me up around eleven the next day. I had lunch scheduled with my dad. George Verduce had flown in from Italy. Another vacation, I suspected. I didn't even know why I bothered with these meetings. They only lasted about thirty minutes, and he'd spend most of his time texting. I'd hoped he'd cancel so I could sleep in.

My driver dropped me off in front of one of the many high-end restaurants my father favored here in the city. I was hardly dressed for the occasion in my untucked button-down, distressed blue jeans, and Converse. I wasn't here to impress.

An attractive leggy hostess held up a blue blazer for me to slip into. She escorted me through the Italian restaurant to Dad's table, which sat in front of an enormous bay window overlooking a courtyard with a running fountain. My old man fit in perfectly with his dark gray Armani suit. His dark espresso hair matched mine, except for a few touches of gray. My longer style was a way better look than that close cut.

"Hey, Dad."

He peered up at me, examined my mismatched blazer, and rolled his eyes.

I took my seat across from him. His attention returned to his phone. *Here we go.*

I thought it wouldn't irritate me as much now that I was in my late twenties, but it did. Still, I appreciated everything he'd done for me. I hadn't worked a day in high school. He gave me pretty much whatever I wanted and had even let me throw the party of the century after I graduated, since he'd missed the ceremony and wanted to make up for it.

"How was Italy?" I asked, breaking the silence between us.

His dark eyes glanced at me from his phone. "Huh? Oh, fine, son. How's everything with you?"

God, this was like déjà vu. Same type of restaurant every month, same half-present conversation. And was that the same suit? Maybe he had fifty of the same one.

I fiddled with the silverware that sat beside the porcelain appetizer plate. "We're probably going to start shooting my band's music video on Monday."

He murmured, "That's great, son," as he continued to tap his cell screen. He was probably working even though he'd just arrived home. One would think he could spare five minutes for his son. I'd never been that lucky.

"I also got a girl pregnant," I drawled.

He nodded. "That's great."

"Yeah, you're gonna be a grandpa," I teased.

That *finally* got his attention. He focused on me again. "Wait, what?"

"Kidding." I grinned.

He shot me a crooked smile. "You little shit." Placing his phone in his pocket, he asked, "So, what're we having?" He looked through the leather-bound menu.

I didn't know why he bothered. He always ordered the same thing: the lobster tail lunch with a side salad.

The waitress approached, a lovely petite brunette. I told her my order.

"I'll have the lobster tail lunch with a side salad," my dad said.

Damn, I'm good.

The meal went as expected. He'd stop eating to answer the phone or respond to a text. But I was used to it. His job had always come first.

"Did you happen to see me on the news?" I asked as the waitress collected our empty plates.

His eyebrows came together. "No. What happened?"

"Got into a fight at the Hard Rock." I wanted to see if he even cared.

Before he could respond, his phone rang. He glanced at the screen. "Sorry, son. I have to take this." He stood and walked away after leaving his credit card on the table.

Typical. Don't know what I expected to be different.

He would probably never change. I hadn't even gotten to tell him about my band's new song. Whatever. I knew where his priorities were. Since Mom had passed away, he hadn't been the same. He couldn't look at me for the first year. Maybe we both just needed to grieve in our own way. It was strange how grief could bring some families together while tearing others apart.

After lunch, Ethan picked me up in a white sedan to go to some theater for dancer auditions.

We were still in bumper-to-bumper traffic when Ethan said, "I have a good feeling about today."

I gave him a narrow-eyed glance. "Why?"

"I think we're finally going to find our girl today," he said, tapping the steering wheel in obvious anticipation.

I cocked an eyebrow. "Do you know something I don't?"

He shook his head. "Of course not."

That usually meant the opposite. I knew that look. Over ten years of friendship told me this asshole had something up his sleeve.

A tingle of dread crept up my spine.

My head throbbed as the sun shone through the windowpanes of my small apartment, straight into my fucking eyes. Blocking the beams with my hand, I lay on the couch in my clothes from last night. My T-shirt still smelled of alcohol. I *desperately* needed a shower.

Mia was cooking in the tiny kitchen, and the scent of coffee filled my nostrils. My feet hit the cool hardwood floor. I honestly didn't know how she wasn't hungover.

"Good morning," she sang, a smile on her face.

"Ugh . . . I hate that you're such a morning person," I said, glancing at the clock hanging on the wall across from me. I'd slept in; it was already eleven. At least it was Saturday. Classes didn't start until four.

"I know." She kept her cheery disposition and served me a plate of scrambled eggs and toast. "I had fun last night."

I grinned. "Good. Mission accomplished." I took a bite. "I don't know if it's the hangover, but this is delicious."

Mia always cooked the perfect scrambled eggs.

She rummaged through the pockets of her jeans and pulled out a business card, then held it up between her index and middle finger.

"Are you gonna show me a magic trick?" I cocked an eyebrow.

"Shut up." She sat next to me. "This is Ethan Miller's contact information."

"Okay?" I still didn't know what the hell she was talking about.

"The band manager of No Blood, No Alibi," she exclaimed, as though the information was common knowledge.

Her high-pitched voice nearly punctured my hungover eardrums. "Why are you so excited about that? He probably just wants to hook up, no offense."

She shot me a glare. "No, bitch. He saw you dancing at the bar last night and thinks you'd be perfect for the band's music video. Apparently, it's a ballad, but he said they're doing most of the shooting in the evenings. The audition is today at one."

I stared at her with a furrowed brow, processing everything, then closed my eyes and picked out the last thing I'd heard: something about Lucas Verduce's band and a music video? I shifted my gaze to the ceiling, looking at the smooth white paint. "Can you repeat that last part?" I leaned forward and placed my empty plate on the thrifted coffee table.

"There's an audition today at one, and I think you should

go." She took my plate to the kitchen and placed it in the sink.

"Why don't *you* go? You're just as good, if not better." I started folding the throw blankets.

She crossed her arms over her chest. "He doesn't want me. He wants *you*. Come on, I'll buy you a cupcake."

What was the worst that could happen?

Silence ensued between us before I heaved a conceding sigh. "Fine. I'll go to the audition, but I want one from Sugar Sweet Sunshine. Not the job I was looking for, but it should pay fairly well, right?"

"And then some."

"Well, if I'm going to make it there on time, I should get ready." I started for the bathroom.

"*We* should get ready."

"You're going?" I stopped, glancing over my shoulder at her from the middle of the hallway.

"Uh, yeah. I'm not going to miss this opportunity to see you in action," she said with a grin.

I didn't want to audition in my ballet attire, so after showering, I threw on black leggings, an oversize sweater, and green Converse. It had been a few years since I'd auditioned for anything. I didn't know the etiquette for these tryouts anymore.

Mia showered and borrowed more of my clothes, dressing more casually this time in jeans, a long-sleeve shirt, and sneakers.

A couple cab rides later, we stopped at Sugar Sweet Sunshine to get Mia her iced coffee and my cupcake, then arrived in front of a red brick structure. Two burly men stood in front of the glass double doors of the theater. There were many girls waiting in the lobby. Mia and I walked up to the entrance only to be stopped by one of the security guards.

His arm shot out, blocking our way inside. "Do you have an invitation?" the tall, bulky man asked.

I realized he was probably talking about that business card. I glanced at Mia, and she pulled Ethan Miller's card from her purse and showed it to him. He took it from her, examined it, and then stepped aside, opening the door for us.

My jaw fell open when I walked into the lobby. An alarming number of beautiful, tall, slim women stood around, waiting for their turn to audition. There I was, little ol' five feet two—three on a good day—with my bun and green Converse. These women portrayed every dance style imaginable, and some were even dressed in their leotards and pointe shoes. Yeah, I didn't stand out at all.

Why did I let Mia talk me into this?

"Are you sure we're at the right audition?" I asked my best friend.

She'd been glancing over at all the women as well. "Um . . . I think so. You know what?" She looked me in the eyes. "They don't want these girls. They *want* you. Just be yourself."

Mia's words eased my jitters. I could always count on her to be my hype woman.

My lips curved up as I murmured, "Thanks, babe."

At that moment, the same dark-haired, blue-eyed man

from the bar walked up to us with a grin on his handsome chiseled features.

"I'm so glad you made it." He glanced at Mia and shot her a wink.

Her face reddened as she gave him a sweet smile. Yep, my best friend was the biggest flirt, even if she didn't want to be.

"Thank you for the opportunity, Mr. Miller." I shook his hand.

"Well, from what I saw last night, I believe you'd be perfect for this role," he said, leading us toward the doors of the main auditorium.

"And you'll love her even more today. Julia is the best dancer you'll find," Mia said, and I really wished she would shut up. I narrowed my eyes at her, telling her to do just that. Her lips quirked up.

Ethan stepped closer to me and canted his head. A corner of his mouth rose.

"What?" Why was he staring at me like I'd done something wrong? Had I offended him last night?

He hesitated and shook his head. "Follow me." He turned on his heel and held the door open to the auditorium.

The seating area was dimly lit, and only the second row, center stage, was full.

Oh god. A mixture of dread and nervousness washed over me. *It's for the kids,* I chanted over and over in my head.

"Good luck, girl," Mia whispered before taking a seat in the back row of the theater.

I followed Ethan down the long carpeted aisle toward

the large stage, my nerves causing a slight tremble in my core. *No turning back now.*

"Do you have a song you want to dance to?" Ethan stopped at the stage steps, which were on the side of the platform.

"I have to tell you something." I glanced over at the row of people, only making out their shadows against the stage lights.

"Okay." He crossed his arms, a hint of concern creeping onto his features.

"I don't know how much Mia told you, but my main style is ballet."

His face turned contemplative. He excused himself to go speak to one of the people in the second row of the dark seating area. I stood there, wondering if I would still be allowed to audition. There were other styles of dance I was versed in, but last night at the bar, I'd basically freestyled to the music.

Ethan walked back over to me. "They want to see what you got."

I released a breath, a mixture of disappointment and relief. Part of me had hoped they wouldn't let me audition. I wasn't a dancer anymore—or I didn't feel like one, anyway. "Okay, 'Diary of Jane' by Breaking Benjamin."

His eyebrows rose as though my song selection surprised him. "Please take the stage."

The spotlight shone on me once I stood center stage. Ethan asked me to introduce myself. I told them my entire name, speaking as loud as I could while rolling up the sleeves of my sweater. They gave me a few seconds to take my starting pose.

When the music started, I was the only person in the auditorium. Everything disappeared from my mind—all my worries, all my cares, all my doubts. My body was in perfect harmony with the melody. The lyrics lured my mind into that emotional place, releasing the disillusionments of my past. My hands roamed up my sides, hips undulating to the rhythm. I pirouetted, one after another, and my heart thrummed against my rib cage as the song ended.

A pin drop could've been heard in the theater. There was only the sound of my rapid breathing. I squinted through the blinding spotlight into the darkness, making sure my audience hadn't left. Nope. They were all still seated in the second row.

Did they like it? Do they still want me? I seriously started to doubt myself.

I made my way off the stage, wondering if I'd blown it. Ethan and Mia met me next to the stage steps with pleased looks on their faces.

"You killed it, Jules," Mia said, giving me an excited smile, her large iced coffee balancing on top of the square cupcake box in her hands.

"Yes, Julia, you did. The producer and the band were all *extremely* impressed with your performance. You're perfect for the part." Ethan winked.

Mia shifted her weight to one leg and said to him, "I told you."

A tall hooded figure stood from the second row and

walked over to us. My eyebrow rose as I leaned my weight onto one leg. The shadows in the dim theater and his dark shades were giving me flashbacks from the night before. Who the hell was this douchebag?

"Ah, here's the lead singer and guitarist of the band," Ethan said, gesturing toward the person.

It wasn't until after he dropped his hood that I realized who he was. Those fucking shades. My nostrils flared, and my heart skipped a beat at the sight of that annoying smirking face.

I glared. "*You.*"

There in front of me stood the unapologetic asshole who'd spilled his drink on me. The fucking guy from the bar.

Without another thought, I grabbed Mia's iced coffee and threw its contents at him, soaking his white shirt and hoodie. I didn't even wait for a reaction before grabbing my cupcake and stomping up the aisle of the theater and walking out.

No regrets.

I stood there like an idiot, my shirt soaked in coffee. Fuck. I wasn't even mad, more amused than anything. I didn't usually get that kind of reaction from women.

Shrugging out of my black hoodie, I noticed Ethan and that notorious coy smirk.

I blew remnants of coffee out my nose. "Did you fucking know who that was?"

He pursed his lips and nodded. "Yep."

"And you still let her audition?" Smug bastard.

He raised his hands in defense. "Hey, it's not my fault you offended her last night. And it's not my fault you can't get over yourself either."

I let out a breath as my bandmates ambled up.

The tall blond rhythm guitarist slapped me on the back. "What the hell did you do, fucker?" Kyle asked. His dark features expressed amusement.

Billy, our dark-haired drummer, slung an arm around my

neck, pulling me down to his level. "Leave it to you to piss off the ideal girl for our video."

I rolled my eyes, pulling out of the headlock.

Our quiet auburn-haired bass player, Mark, just looked at me and shook his head.

Lita strolled up, her tight brown curls bouncing with each step. "She's fuckin' hot. I like that half sleeve of cherry blossoms on her arm."

"I doubt she bats for your team." Kyle grinned.

Lita straightened her black tank top and held her tattooed arm, leaning her curvy body on one leg. "Hell, she probably swings both ways. My sixth sense is tingling." She stuck her hands into the pockets of her baggy black cargo pants, looking like she was straight out of the '90s. She pulled off that Avril Lavigne look well.

Ethan changed the subject, obviously annoyed by the whole situation. "Okay, guys, enough."

"There are more women waiting," Mark chimed in, examining his nails like he was bored.

The producer, Mr. Jameson, approached at a slinking pace in his bespoke suit. His brow furrowed as he looked at me. "I don't know what you did to piss her off, Verduce, but she's fucking perfect for the video. Love her look, love her dancing. She's everything. Whatever you did, *fix* it."

Of course he would fucking love her.

I let out a breath, dread trickling up my spine.

Mr. Jameson rolled his shoulders. "Get her back. Put an offer on the table she can't refuse."

Fuck me. I really didn't want to deal with that woman

again. *Maybe I should put on a raincoat before going to meet her.* All eyes were on me at this point.

"Fine, I'll fix it."

"Good boy," Mr. Jameson said, and the motherfucker had the audacity to pat me on the head.

He was so lucky he ran this shit. Otherwise, my fist would've ended up in his face.

He started to stroll out of the auditorium, taking his entourage with him. "We start shooting Monday. So, chop-chop."

"A lot of fucking help you guys are." I turned to my bandmates and Ethan. "Why can't one of you talk to her? She obviously wants nothing to do with me." I gestured to the coffee stain on my shirt.

Lita held up her hands, palms facing me. "This is your shit show, dude. I'm just the keyboard player," she said before making a straight line for the exit.

"You're the reason she doesn't want the job. You should compromise," Mark said in his monotone voice.

There was no fucking way that chick would compromise. He was off his rocker.

Billy chimed in, "Maybe we can scare her into a contract."

Ethan and Kyle shook their heads in complete disapproval.

"Fuck me." I let out a long sigh and looked to Ethan. "Fine, what do you know about her?"

He appeared surprised by the question. "Not much. Just that her best friend, Mia, works for her."

"Doing?" I prodded.

"Fuck if I know." He tossed his arms up into the air.

How the hell was I going to find this chick? I groaned, placed my hands on top of my head, interlaced my fingers, and peered at the dark ceiling panels. We usually had the dancers' information on file, but Julia had been an impromptu audition. We didn't have time to go through the list of Julia Blackwells in NYC.

"Wait," Ethan said, a contemplative expression on his face.

I shot him a hopeful look. "What?"

Ethan lifted his index finger as though he'd had an epiphany. "Mia said they knew the band members playing at the bar last night."

"Great. Find out the name of that band and where they're playing next. We'll start there," I said.

Kyle asked, "Can I go?"

I narrowed my eyes. "You just want to go for the chicks."

He didn't have the best track record with women. Worse than mine, actually. Could I trust him not to fuck things up?

He shrugged. "And for moral support."

"Whatever, yeah. Let's get out of here. I need a drink," I said.

Ethan walked into the lobby and disappointed the rest of the women, telling them the position had been filled.

A ride back to my penthouse and a few phone calls later, Ethan acquired the next gig location of In Your Head. They would be playing at a bar in Lower Manhattan. I changed out of my coffee-stained shirt, then Ethan, Kyle, and I headed out.

I hoped one of their band members would be willing to share anything about this Julia chick. Hell, I really hoped it wouldn't cause another bar fight. I needed to stay out of the media's eye.

THE OUTSIDE OF THE BAR WAS DECEIVING. IT LOOKED like an old grocery store that'd been painted red. On the inside, there were many pops of color, and it was more spacious than the one they'd played at the night before. I hadn't been here before, but I liked it. I glanced at each of the members on the elevated stage. It was a diverse group, which I appreciated. They were in the middle of setting up.

Of course, the staff recognized us immediately. Ethan always had our security in mind everywhere we went. My usual bodyguard, Chris, and two other tall, burly guys trailed behind us.

The gorgeous bleach-blond woman walked in from the back and glanced at our group. "Lucas V? I'm a huge fan," she said, walking over to us. We shook hands, and she greeted Ethan. She turned her dark eyes to Kyle. "Man, you can really shred. Love your riffs."

"Please, don't inflate his ego anymore," I half joked.

She placed her hands on her hips. "So, what brings you guys out here?"

I stared at her for a moment, noticing the black eyeliner around her brown eyes. *Should I just come out and ask about Julia, or would it be more beneficial to stay and watch them perform first?* I nudged Ethan with my gaze, letting him take the reins.

He shot me a glare of disdain before turning back to the woman. "Well, Miss—"

"Just call me Gale." A suspicious expression crept onto her lovely features.

Ethan let out a sharp breath. "We're actually looking for someone by the name of Julia Blackwell."

She crossed her arms, and as she was about to respond, a dark-haired man a few inches taller than her walked over. "Oh, shit. Lucas Verduce and Kyle Jones. What the fuck are you guys doing here?" He seemed like he could be older than all of his bandmates, but I couldn't tell. This guy hid his age well.

"This is our drummer, Rick," Gale said before turning to him. "They're looking for Julia."

Rick's eyebrows wrinkled. "What do you want with her?"

Great. I instantly sensed the protective vibe between these two. Either they were her parents or really good friends. Didn't know how to tell. I also didn't know how to explain the situation to them. Julia wanted nothing to do with me. She'd made that much clear. My mind flashed back to the look of contempt on her face as she tossed that iced coffee on me. The thought made me grin. God, I was a sick fuck.

"We have some business to conduct with her," Ethan said.

Gale cocked an eyebrow.

Motherfucker. I hoped they didn't take that the wrong way. He'd made it sound like maybe she was doing something illegal. I shot my manager a wide-eyed look, like I was saying, "You better correct yourself, fucker."

"It's not anything bad," Kyle added, and I wasn't sure if he'd made the situation better or not.

Rick crossed his arms, his lips thinning into a hardened line.

Shit, I should've come alone. These guys weren't helping at all. "We're shooting a music video, and my producer loved her audition. We have an offer for her."

Gale and Rick exchanged glances. They obviously knew her or knew of her.

"Excuse us." Gale pulled Rick far enough away that we couldn't hear them.

"How do you think Julia knows them?" Ethan whispered.

I shrugged, then stared at Rick for a second. He had Julia's eyes and nose. "He could be her brother or something."

"Gale's kind of hot," Kyle remarked, his eyes roaming her curves.

With an eye roll, I said, "Fucking stay away from her, man. Those two look like they might have a thing. Don't fuck this up."

"That's never stopped me before." Kyle smirked.

I was going to have to hurt him.

Gale and Rick made their way back over to us after a very animated conversation with each other.

"Okay, here's the deal. Our guitarist played hooky tonight. We need someone on rhythm," Rick said in his deep voice. "You do this for us, and I'll give you an address."

That wasn't such a terrible trade. I held my hand out. "Deal."

Rick gripped it firmly, sealing our bargain. "Let's go get you set up. Gale can give you the music."

"Hope you can keep up, kid," she said. A corner of her lips quirked.

I grinned. It'd been a while since I'd played with a completely different band. From what I'd heard the night before, they performed similar-sounding music to No Blood, No Alibi. How difficult could playing with them be?

Ethan pulled me off to the side before I could step onstage. "Are you sure this is a good idea? This is going to be all over social media within minutes."

"Then I guess you'd better call for more security." I placed a heavy hand on his shoulder. "You got a better plan?"

He shot me a defeated look and took a step back, saying nothing.

"Don't worry, I don't plan on going to jail tonight," I said before walking up the two steps onto the stage.

"That's very reassuring, asshole," he bellowed after me.

I pretended not to hear him so it would piss him off even more.

That night, In Your Head earned my respect and admiration. Gale introduced me as a substitute, and the audience went crazy. Rick's performance on the drums was wild. He didn't miss a fucking beat. Gale shredded on the guitar enough to even put Kyle to shame. All the cues were on point, and the mistakes—if there were any—were hardly noticeable. When we performed a cover of one of the popular mainstream songs, they made it sound like it was their own. The bar filled to capacity quickly. Everyone danced and sang along to the lyrics.

After the final set, Gale and Rick pulled me backstage with them. Ethan and Kyle were waiting with two bodyguards. The crowd had become a bit unruly, especially with all the alcohol intake. Some people tried to sneak backstage, but my security took care of that.

"I have a car waiting for us out back," Ethan said, checking his Apple Watch.

The two bulky bodyguards stood next to the stage door exit, ready to get us the hell out of there. I needed to get the information I'd been promised first.

"You did all right, Verduce." Rick wrote something down on the back of their band's promo flier and gave it to me.

"You were epic, Gale. I could probably learn a lot from you," Kyle said, looking at her with admiration and heat in his blue eyes.

She nodded and smirked. "Yeah, you probably could."

"We need to go," Ethan prodded as the audience chanted for an encore. I knew we didn't have time for one.

Before I could walk out, Rick said low enough that only I

could hear, "I hope this project of yours is short. She's not into long-term gigs, if you catch my drift."

"It's only a month of shooting," I said, intrigued by his statement.

"Treat my Jay Bird right. You better not screw her over."

I lifted a brow. "So . . . you're her dad, then?"

"Don't I look like it?" He grinned.

Ethan tugged my arm. We rushed out of the building like it was on fire. People were gathering outside, surrounding the SUV we were supposed to be riding in. The bodyguards did their job and cleared a path for us to get in safely.

The ride back to my penthouse was silent as I shone my cell light on the flier Rick had given me, staring at the address written in black Sharpie. *This is it.*

CHAPTER 6

Julia

Sure, I probably could've been more civilized about rejecting the offer. Dad always said I had a bad temper. There was just something about Lucas's russet eyes that set my insides on fire in the worst way possible.

Mia had scolded me for throwing her iced coffee on him. I didn't know why, but she never finished them.

My stomach grumbled as I concluded a ballet class with my second group of students for the day. That meant it was time to eat.

After the last of my students filed out, Mia padded out of the back office, shaking a large square container of salad. "I received another text from the theater manager. We really should invest in a business phone."

He'd been trying to get ahold of me on my cell as well. I wasn't ready to confront him about the payment though.

I let out a breath. "I know. Guess I'll check out the nearby bars. Maybe they can use a cocktail waitress."

Mia peered out the panoramic studio window. "Are you expecting visitors?"

An expensive blacked-out SUV was parked right outside my building, next to the curb. Luckily, all my students had left, so there was no one to hear me say, "What the fuck?"

Ethan stepped out of the vehicle and walked around to open the other door. Lucas climbed out wearing a fitted tee, jeans, and sneakers. He looked so fucking good, I wanted to slap him. When had I become so violent?

My first instinct was to lock the door, but there was no time. God, I was such a bitch. I had time to rush behind the reception desk and duck beneath the small space as the bells on my door jingled. I could only imagine what Mia thought and the look of amusement on her face.

"Ethan. Lucas. What are you two doing here?" Mia asked, a hint of nervousness in her voice.

"Mia, nice to see you again," Ethan said in an upbeat tone. He was probably a morning person, like her. "So, this is where you work," he muttered.

"Yup." The nervousness faded from her voice. "What can I do for you?"

"I think you know who we're looking for," Lucas crooned in his smooth tenor tone. "Where is she?"

Could I just stand—or crouch—there and listen to them interrogate Mia? She didn't deserve that.

For fuck's sake. With my heart barreling out of my chest and a not-so-calming breath, I stood up from behind the desk, ready to kick them out of my studio. The two men stood there with amused expressions on their gorgeous faces, making my blood boil even more.

"Nice of you to pop in," Lucas said, leaning his forearms on the raised part of the desk, his cedar-and-vanilla scent filling my nostrils.

I gritted my teeth, hating his arrogance. It made me want to throat punch him.

Jesus, he was better looking than I'd expected without the fucking shades. *So annoying.* How the hell had I missed that slightly off-center lip ring on that smart-ass mouth? "Wish I could say the same of you. What do you want?" I asked.

Ethan cleared his throat. "The producer loved your audition. He insists on having you in the music video."

This was my chance to get the money for the theater payment. I just needed to play my cards right.

"Huh, that's too bad," I said, folding my arms over my chest.

Lucas leaned in closer, his tatted, toned body coming halfway across the desk. "Listen, Sunshine, we have an offer you *can't* refuse." His soft minty breath brushed over my warm cheeks.

I took a step back, putting distance between us. "I highly doubt that."

"Maybe you should hear what they have to say, Jules." Mia shrugged.

Ethan added, "You won't regret it."

They had me pinned in the corner like some kind of helpless prey. I rolled my eyes. "I'm sure."

Lucas straightened and crossed his arms. "Is there somewhere the two of us can talk? In private?"

My feet went into motion toward the back. "You have five minutes." He had less than that. I didn't want to be alone in a room with this man longer than I needed to.

After leading him into the small back office, which had no windows and bare white walls, I closed the door. The desk was built into one side of the narrow room, taking up most of the space.

I leaned against the edge and tapped my watch. "Okay, talk."

Lucas grinned as he flicked his lip ring with his tongue, and I really wished he wouldn't look at me like that.

He took a step toward me, his gaze wandering the small area. "Do you own this studio?"

I flinched as he moved closer. *Why did I do that?*

His smile widened.

"I'm leasing it. Why?" I asked, staying focused on the conversation and not his proximity.

"Just curious." His eyes shifted to the only picture in my office: me, my dad, and Gale at my Juilliard graduation ceremony.

"This is kinda small for a ballet studio, isn't it?" he said.

I wondered why he was asking so many questions. "So?" My patience was dwindling.

It was true that I was running out of space for students. Even with a full roster, my business had been barely making it. *Fucking rock stars.*

His eyes roamed over my body, and the heat in my core rose.

"Why ballet?" He stepped in front of me, leaned down, and placed his arms on either side of me, his hands bracing against the edge of the desk.

There was nowhere else to go in this tiny fucking office. His vanilla-and-cedar scent invaded the space between us. My muscles tensed when he brought his face a hairsbreadth from mine.

"What kind of question is that? You have less than three minutes to tell me what the fuck you want."

His gaze flicked from my lips to my eyes. "What will it take for you to do this music video with me?"

This guy wasn't used to not getting his way.

I have him right where I want him.

I accidentally swiped an open manila envelope onto the floor when I lifted my hand to push him away. The programs for my recital scattered onto the white tile. Lucas immediately crouched down to pick them up. Once he'd gathered the programs, he peered up at me. Our eyes locked.

Or maybe this is where I want him.

His eyebrow rose. "Spring dance recital?"

"Yes," I hissed, snatching the papers away from him and placing them with the rest of the copies. "I believe your five minutes are up."

Not a moment later, Ethan burst into the room and stared at us with a cocked eyebrow. "I told you to do whatever it takes, but I didn't mean this."

Lucas straightened. "Haha, asshole."

Ethan chuckled and walked away, leaving the door open.

After laying the envelope back on the desk, Lucas stared at me, determination and heat in his eyes.

I swallowed and held my ground. He leaned back against the doorframe, arms crossed.

"Why do you dislike me so much?" he asked.

My eyes narrowed. "Let me count the ways. You're rude, arrogant, overprivileged—"

He smirked. "Don't forget sinfully good-looking and a stallion between the sheets."

My nostrils flared. "Meeting's over, rock star."

"We can pay for whatever you need." He'd said it like it was no big deal, but my bills weren't cheap.

He has to know that, right?

He must've been *really* desperate. And I wondered how desperate. Should I have been flattered or offended? He was basically trying to pay for me. More like pay for my . . . dancing services?

I looked up at him and stepped closer. "Why me? What about the other girls who auditioned?"

Lucas studied me. "Ethan dismissed them. Look, the producer loves everything about you, and he wants *you* for the part."

My lips curved up. "So, basically, you're his bitch boy."

A muscle in his jaw ticked. "No, I'm his employee."

I knew that would get under his skin. But I wasn't going to settle for what he was offering me. "I want four hundred a day."

"What?"

"You heard me. My time is precious."

Irritation seeped through his hardened expression, and his arms loosened over his chest. "Three hundred a day."

"Three fifty."

He let out a sigh, tilting his head up before meeting my gaze once more. His eyes lingered on me before he said, "Done."

It was too fucking hot in that room, and the way he stared at me made me want to—no. I couldn't be attracted to this asshole. I *refused* to be attracted to him. "Good. We're done here."

He flicked that fucking lip ring with his tongue again before that devilish smirk crept onto his face. "Pleasure doing business with you, Sunshine."

God, had I just made a deal with the devil?

My jaw clenched as he turned and walked out of the office. Rolling the tension from my shoulders, I trailed behind. Mia and Ethan scrambled to the front of the reception desk, silent as they looked our way, grinning wide. It was obvious they'd been eavesdropping.

Lucas strode up to Ethan. "Go over the contract with her." He turned to me and said, "Shooting starts tomorrow."

What the hell? I needed more time to make arrangements with my individual lessons. "That's such short notice."

"If you have an issue with it, talk to the producer. I doubt he'll accommodate you," Lucas said as he typed something on his smartphone.

"I can already tell working with you is gonna be a

fucking joy," I said, turning on my heel, striding into my office, and slamming the door behind me. I took three deep calming breaths.

It's for the kids. It's for the kids. It's for the kids.

THANKFULLY, MY JOB KEPT MY MIND OFF THE EVENTS that had occurred earlier that afternoon. I was stacked with private lessons and loved every moment with those kiddos. After the last session of the evening, Mia and I did a few stretching exercises in front of the mirrors of the studio, then sprawled out on the cool floor, staring up at the ugly white ceiling tiles.

"Today was quite eventful," she said, breaking the silence with her cheerful honey voice.

"Yep," I muttered, wanting to forget everything that had happened with Lucas. God, he was insufferable. "I really *don't* want to talk about it."

Mia smirked. "Why not? Did something happen between you two before Ethan barged in?"

I scrunched my nose. "Fuck no. Nothing happened. Less than nothing."

She smacked my bicep. "You cuss a lot for a ballerina. I'm surprised your tongue doesn't slip during lessons."

That couldn't be helped. My dad hadn't believed in censoring cuss words after Mom left. "Trust me, sometimes I have to bite it."

She turned and propped her head on her hand. "Anyway, Lucas is a fucking hottie."

Way to state the obvious. I turned my head and stared into her big brown eyes. "Who's the potty mouth now?"

She smacked me again. "Stop changing the subject."

I intertwined my hands on my stomach. "He may be hot, but that doesn't make up for his shitty personality. Asshole isn't my type."

Her eyes narrowed a bit. "So, you're saying you *wouldn't* use him for sex? How long has it been? You're letting that IUD go to waste."

My jaw dropped. "Hey, I've been busy with all of this." I gestured to the whole studio space. "And no. I wouldn't want to fuck that dirty dick of his."

She giggled.

"Besides, I don't have time for a fuckboy. They say the first two years of starting a business are the hardest," I said.

"Well, what about Shawn? Didn't you sleep with him?"

"You know I don't count anyone who can't make me come."

"That's sad. No wonder you ghosted him." A few seconds passed before she heaved a sigh. "Seriously Jules, maybe you need to make time for a love life. What're you gonna do when your studio is doing well and you don't have to be here as much?"

I honestly hadn't thought that far. "Hang out with you more?"

"No, bitch. I'll probably be married with kids by then.

Unless you're volunteering yourself for babysitting duty?" she said.

After what my mom had put my dad through, I wasn't even sure I could see that kind of future with anyone. Besides, teaching ballet kept me content. Happy. It did . . . Really . . .

Her voice took on a solemn tone. "I want you to be happy. Whether you find it with someone or not."

"How do you know I'm not happy now?"

She deadpanned, "I know you're tired, Jules. Tired of doing everything yourself. Tired of relying on *only* yourself for everything. You have no one to depend on but me."

"You're all I need."

Mia shook her head. "Yeah, but you pay me."

My brow furrowed. "Are you telling me we're only best friends because I'm paying you?"

She shot me a toothy smile. "No! But it helps."

I rolled my eyes. Mia Cruz had been the most reliable person in my life.

Maybe I did want to share my life with someone, but I didn't think that someone was Lucas Verduce.

CHAPTER 7

Lucas

Another fucking music video. This would make the fourth one in my career, and so far, I'd hated shooting every one of them. I really hoped the director would take a different approach to this one, mostly because all the scenes were generic and typical of a rock music video. The song itself was more on the romantic side. Our band had never been the ballad type—until our record sales dropped and the record company practically threw these lyrics at us.

Whatever. I was ready to get this over with. It was after five, and we were running late. Ethan had done everything in his power to shove me out of the penthouse through the crowd of fans gathered in front of the building.

He sat next to me as the chauffeur drove us to the shoot location. "We can't be on time for anything, I swear," he muttered, tapping the screen of his Apple Watch.

I propped my elbow on the door. "Did you send a car to pick Julia up?"

"Yeah. She's probably already there," he replied, staring out the tinted window. The windows of the SUV were so dark that it looked like a crypt inside.

"Great," I muttered.

She hadn't made anything easy and wasn't the type to back down from a difficult situation; she'd proven that much when we were alone in her office. I could only imagine what it'd be like shooting this music video.

My dick betrayed me, stirring in my jeans at the thought of her staring up at me with those gorgeous dark almond-shaped eyes. Her high cheekbones, that cute nose, and those full, plump lips. Fuck. Why'd she have to be so fucking gorgeous?

Ethan turned his head to look at me with a firm expression on his features. "Not that I think it'll happen, but you know to keep things professional with her, right? Also, if the song is a hit, you'll be going on tour. US only."

Fuck. My eyebrows wrinkled. "I never agreed to that."

He stared at me for a moment. "Come on, man. You act like you don't want thousands of girls after your dick anymore."

Well . . . it was because I didn't. The relationships I'd had with all those women were shallow. At the beginning of the year, my tolerance for them had decreased. I wanted more, and maybe I hadn't wanted to admit that until now.

The only reason I'd agreed to everything over the past year was because my bandmates wanted to jump on the opportunity. They'd likely want to go on tour, and I didn't want to disappoint them. So, what choice did I have?

After security checked us at the gate, we pulled into the circular gravel driveway of a huge mansion. The production crew had already begun the setup process. White pillars lined the brick porch, the windows gave me a cottage vibe, and green vines climbed half the structure. People scrambled in and out of the wide front door.

Ethan and I exited the SUV. We walked in and were immediately met by a team of people. The director, Katie Smith, walked up with her hands on her hips, headphones hanging around her neck. She did not look pleased.

"Where the hell have you been?" the blond-haired woman asked. "You're so lucky your counterpart is the one doing all the work in this scene. You just have to sit there and look pretty."

I grinned at Katie, who wore high-top sneakers, jeans, and V-neck tee. "Thought that's why I was here in the first place."

Her nostrils flared. "Ethan, make sure he's ready in thirty. We're going to be here all night," she muttered as Ethan led me to where wardrobe, hair, and makeup was setup. I hadn't seen Julia yet. Ethan told me she was on set learning the choreography.

The song, "My Crimson Love," was about the crazy, violent, passionate side of what love could be. Katie had briefly gone over the scenes she had in mind for the song in our preproduction meeting. She'd talked about a sexy bed scene.

That would be interesting. I'd been in bed with a lot of chicks, but never with one who didn't want to be there. Not that I'd be fucking Julia for real. Shit, she was probably limber, and the thought of having hate sex with her had my dick at half-mast.

Fuck, I didn't want to get a full hard-on in front of this wardrobe chick, so I thought of something else. Anything else. God, why was Julia such a fucking turn-on?

Wardrobe dressed me in a black Henley and jeans that hung off my waist. Hair and makeup double-teamed me, and within twenty minutes, I was ready to go.

My feet were bare and cold as I walked on set into the huge living room. Oak-paneled walls and dark hardwood floors complemented the light-colored furniture in the space. A large flat screen hung above the fireplace mantel. Katie told me to sit on the plush couch that had been set up in front of the TV.

Julia walked out shortly after me, and *holy fuck.*

She stood there barefoot, clad in a long red satin robe with long sleeves. Her tan dancer's legs were on full display through the front slit, long onyx hair styled in soft waves down her shoulders. Makeup darkened her eyes, and she wore burgundy lipstick. I wanted to smear it with my mouth and bite that full bottom lip of hers.

A hint of black lingerie and cleavage showed above where the robe was tied together. My dick stirred.

Down, boy. I attempted to look as disinterested as I could while sitting on the couch. Wasn't entirely sure if I was succeeding. It didn't help that it had been a while since I'd fucked anyone. I'd been busy recording the new song and trying to find inspiration for lyrics that weren't the record company's. Thank God our contract was almost over. Granted, I wasn't entirely sure where I wanted to go or what I wanted to do after.

Katie walked on set and said, "Okay, Julia, you're trying to get his attention. It's been a long day, and you're ready for some lovemaking. We're going to zoom in on Lucas singing first. You know your cue, Julia."

Julia nodded, appearing calm as could be.

How the hell was she not nervous? Probably from years of performing. God, she exuded confidence and professionalism. Fuck, I was in trouble. I couldn't stop staring. She was so focused on the scene, and all I could think about was running my hands over her silky skin like some fucking horny teenager. Mentally, I palmed my forehead.

Once the director walked off set, Julia caught me staring and shot me a glare. I wanted nothing more than to fuck that attitude right out of her. It was probably sick of me to have the hots for someone who hated my guts.

The music began to play, and I started lip-synching to the lyrics. Katie cued Julia to start dancing, and fuck was it difficult not to get distracted. Her movements were so fluid and seamless. I was supposed to be ignoring her. It was so. Fucking. Hard. *Pun intended.*

"Cut," Katie exclaimed. "Lucas, you need to look bored and unamused. The opposite of how you look now."

Fuck her for calling me out like that. My gaze went to Julia's face, and her dark eyes focused on me as her lips curved up. *So smug.* I was going to get her back for this.

"Got it," I grunted.

"Okay, continue with the scene. Roll it!"

Julia moved to the melodic rhythm of the acoustic guitar. Her hips shimmied to the beat of the drums as she dropped to her knees and started crawling toward me on her hands and knees. Her dark eyes met mine, and my dick strained against my jeans. She closed in, running her hands up my shins. They ended on my thighs as she snaked her body up mine and straddled me. Her skin was warm and damp with perspiration. Her lavender scent mixed with the movement of her tantalizing hips elicited a rumble in my chest. I gritted my teeth, attempting to keep my face stoic. Couldn't let her know the effect she was having on me.

The lyrics started, and for the first time in my career, I fucking missed my cue. A corner of Julia's mouth rose. I gripped her hips and pulled her firmly against my hard-on, letting her feel what she was doing to me. Her eyes widened, breath hitching.

Katie pinched the bridge of her nose, a look of annoyance on her face. "Cut! Lucas, stop dicking around. The sooner we wrap this scene, the sooner we can move on."

"Sorry, boss," I said, my attention still on Julia.

"Cut the *boss* crap," Katie shot back.

The song started a couple seconds before the lyrics began. I didn't miss my cue this time. Julia tugged the string of her robe while I sang. It fell open, revealing black lace covering her breasts.

Were her nipples hard? Maybe I was affecting her more than I knew.

Fuck. Focus, Verduce. She's so fucking soft. The silky material fell down one of her shoulders. My hands roamed to the bare skin of her waist, and before I could stop myself, I thrust my hardness up between her legs.

"More of that," Katie said through the music.

Thankfully, I didn't have to lip-synch anymore and was able to focus on the gorgeous woman on my lap. My blood pulsed in my ears as she bit her lip, gyrating her hips to the rhythm. Her lace-clad pussy occasionally skimmed my dick through my pants. She danced her way off my lap and performed a move where she stretched her legs out into the perfect splits. My dick throbbed. I was going to need a lot of lube and a long jerk session.

After several takes, the torture finally ended when the director yelled, "Wrap it up for the night."

What the fuck was that? I wasted no time getting the fuck off set, making my way back to wardrobe. I'd shot raunchier scenes with supermodels, so why was my body betraying me like this? I used a makeup wipe to remove the black eyeliner from around my eyes.

Julia had acted like it didn't even faze her. She was either very good at performing or just hated me that much. Had she felt anything or gotten aroused a little? That woman was difficult to read, and it was starting to drive me insane.

"Well, that was fun."

I glanced up at Ethan through the vanity mirror. He leaned against the doorframe with his arms crossed.

"Yeah," I muttered, grabbing another wipe and

continuing to remove the shit from my face. He was grinning. Why was the motherfucker grinning? "What?"

He stepped closer. "You know *what*. You missed your cue."

"I know."

"You lost focus."

"I know."

Ethan still had that stupid smile on his face. "I don't think I've seen anyone have that kind of effect on you."

Fuck. If he'd noticed, that meant everyone on set knew. It was only a matter of time before my fucking bandmates would know. I couldn't let this chick get to me. Next time, I'd be better prepared. "Moment of weakness."

"Right." He dragged out the word. "I'll be in the car." In saying that, he walked out.

I stared at myself in the mirror, determined to get over the infatuation I had with that woman. It was going to be like any other shoot I'd worked on, and I only had to endure three more weeks of this shit.

CHAPTER 8

Julia

Rough guitar-calloused fingers on my hips. Dark russet eyes filled with carnal promise. The bulge in his jeans grinding against my lace-covered pussy. How I'd managed to keep my resting bitch face was beyond me. Had Lucas felt my heart racing? Had he noticed my shallow breaths? The flush of my cheeks? It probably didn't help that I'd been focused on performing difficult movements. Though the choreography had been fairly easy to memorize.

"Earth to Julia," Mia shouted from across the ballet studio.

My mind snapped back to reality as I met her stare in the mirror. "What?"

"What were you thinking about?" she asked, amused.

"Nothing." I knew she would prod; my response had been way too quick.

She tilted her head to the side, studying me from behind the reception desk. I had thirty minutes until my next class. I picked up the white cloth and Windex and sprayed the mirror, then wiped it down.

"Were you thinking dirty thoughts?" Mia asked, a hint of accusation in her sweet voice.

My nose scrunched. "No."

She grinned. "Liar. You were biting your lip and blushing. That usually means you're thinking dirty thoughts."

I looked away and continued with what I was doing. "You're ridiculous."

"I take it last night's shoot went well," she said.

What was I supposed to say? That I nearly got off simply by dry humping Lucas Verduce? No. I refused to give in to his rock star charms. "It went okay."

She huffed and rolled her eyes at me. My studio and students came first above all else. I couldn't afford any distractions at this point in my career.

"Do you know what scene you're doing tonight?" Mia asked, stepping out from behind the desk and leaning against the front of it.

I continued to the next mirror panel. "Lucas and I have a dance scene together. I think we're going to be learning the choreography for the next few days. It's supposedly a more complicated routine. As long as it doesn't involve me giving him a lap dance again, I'm good." I shivered.

Mia squealed. "Excuse me?" She stomped closer to me, her brown eyes wide. "You did what?"

"Oh, shit. Did I say that out loud?" My cheeks warmed. *So annoying.* "It's not a big deal, M."

She laughed. "Bitch. No big deal? You fucking gave Lucas Verduce a lap dance, and it's no big deal? You're so full of shit."

With a shrug, I replied, "There were other people in the room. It's not like we fucked."

She stood there with her hands on her hips and deadpanned, "Stop trying to downplay this."

"Are you mad I gave him a lap dance?"

"I'm not mad. I just don't want you to clam up on me while you're going through all of this. I know it has to be overwhelming for you," she said, concern washing over her features.

"I don't clam up." Irritation seeped from my voice.

"Yes, you do. It's okay to feel something other than rage, Jules."

Tears seemed like a waste of time. Life was a whole lot easier when I got angry. "Really, it's not a big deal."

"There are millions of girls who would pay to give him a lap dance. Trust me, it's something," she said.

A few students trickled into the studio, bringing our conversation to a halt. Mia gave me that look that said we would continue our discussion later, but there wasn't anything else to talk about. I'd just danced, ground against, and aroused *the* Lucas Verduce. Okay. Maybe I was delusional. Maybe I was downplaying it. But it didn't mean anything. I wouldn't let it.

Right after my last class, I went to the back office to change into casual clothes. I pulled on my ripped boyfriend-style jeans and plaid button-down and slid into my black Converse. My cell phone rang while I finished tying my shoes.

Why the hell is Dad calling me? He never calls me.

"Dad, everything okay?" I asked, trying not to sound panicked.

"Oh yeah, everything's fine, Jay Bird—"

"Hey, Jules," Gale said. They probably had me on speaker.

Dad continued, "We were wondering if you had a visit from a certain rock star yet."

Well, shit, how the hell did they know about Lucas? That damn Lucas was a determined motherfucker. "You snitched on me, Dad? How could you?" I'd wondered how the hell he'd found me.

"He was quite persistent. We made him play with the band in exchange for your address," Gale said.

"You pimped me out?" I raised my voice.

"It was your father's idea," Gale said.

"Thanks for throwing me under the bus, ass," he said.

"Please, you crawled under there when you made the agreement," she retorted.

Amused at their bickering, I said, "I wish you two would get together already, or at least hook up."

Silence ensued for a second before Gale said, "Your dad couldn't handle all this, babe."

I laughed.

"Anyway," Dad interjected, "what happened with the rock star?"

I let out a breath. "I signed a contract to dance in his music video."

"Did you read it thoroughly?" he asked.

Had I? Of course I had. Well, did skimming count? I supposed I should have consulted my dad before signing it, but I'd really wanted Lucas and Ethan out of my studio at that moment.

"Jay Bird?"

"Yes, Dad. I'm not stupid." Hopefully. Shit. *I hope I didn't miss anything important.*

Just then, Mia called from the front. The car was waiting to take me to the video shoot.

"I have to go, Dad. I'll give you details later." With that, I hung up the phone, grabbed my tote, and rushed out the door of my studio, bidding Mia goodbye. With my new work schedule, she would have to get used to locking up the place.

The sunset on the horizon framed the gorgeous Southampton mansion as our black sedan drove up the long driveway. I hopped out of the car once we'd stopped in the crowded entry and rushed through the front door. With a strangled grunt, I bumped someone in the entryway, causing a chain reaction of events that resulted in some toppled lighting equipment and fallen chairs.

"Shit," I wanted to disappear. "I'm so sorry."

The girl I'd accidentally knocked to the ground said, "I didn't see you."

What a time to be clumsy. I helped her up as a few crew

members stared daggers at me for the mess I'd caused. "No, it's totally my fault."

A familiar voice sounded from behind me. "Great going, Sunshine."

The crew and that poor girl continued to pick up the mess. Thankfully, none of the equipment had broken, and more importantly, no one was hurt. *No harm, no foul.* I turned to face the bane of my existence.

Lucas wore a white muscle shirt that showed off his toned tatted arms and shoulders. His jeans hung low on his hips, and he was barefoot again.

"It was an accident," I snapped. "And I apologized, unlike *some* people around here."

He flicked that fucking lip ring of his. "Hmm . . . that *does* sound familiar."

Don't let him get to you. "Is there a reason you're talking to me?" I managed to ask in a calm manner.

The corner of his mouth rose, and I instantly wanted to kick him in his shin. "The choreographer's waiting for us in the other room."

"Lead the way," I said with an exaggerated sweeping hand gesture.

We ambled down the wide hallway to a room with beautiful paned windows and oak-paneled walls. The crew had turned the library into a makeshift dance studio, lining one wall with rolling mirror panels. In front of those mirrors stood the choreographer, Alfredo Leto, barefoot and clad in all black.

"What? You're going to dance in that?" Alfredo was dramatic. Everything about him screamed *diva*.

I nodded.

"Take off your shoes at least. I want you to be grounded," he said, walking over to the large wireless speaker on the desk.

With a conceding sigh, I slipped off my Converse and socks, revealing my unpainted toenails. The calluses on my feet weren't as bad as they used to be, but I was still *very* self-conscious about them. I caught Lucas staring at them.

"Stop it," I said, pushing past him to where Alfredo stood in front of the mirrors.

"Miss Katie says this dance between you two should be full of aggression and passion," Alfredo said, standing beside me, facing the mirror. "Let's go, rock star. We don't have all night."

I learned two things about Lucas Verduce that night: he couldn't dance for shit, and he had the hip thrusting down. God, did he have it down. My mind wandered to a place it shouldn't have. This guy was an asshole, but still *very* fuckable. I never bothered with the type, even if it was just sex.

Alfredo first went over the steps without music, slow and steady. That didn't seem like a problem for Lucas. But when the music played, he couldn't keep the rhythm to save his life.

We went through the routine for the millionth time, my patience wearing thin as he stepped on my foot yet again. "Oh my god, why can't you get this right?" I snapped.

"Fuck, I'm sorry. I'm trying." He brushed his fingers through his dark hair, frustration apparent on his face.

I demonstrated the sweeping movement. "It's one, two, three and four."

"Look, I'm not a fucking dancer. This is stupid. Can't we eighty-six this scene?" He looked at the amused Alfredo.

"Afraid not, rock star. The director has a vision, and unless you can come up with a better one, you two will just have to deal with this." Alfredo gestured to both of us.

Lucas ran his palms down his face as I let out a breath, rolling the tension from my shoulders.

"You two seem to have great chemistry. I really don't know what the problem is here." Alfredo examined his manicured hand.

That is the problem. I crossed my arms and scoffed, "The problem is he's an asshole."

Lucas's gaze narrowed on me. "I could say the same about you."

"You did not call me an asshole." It was probably juvenile and immature, but I shoved him.

"Okay. Okay." Alfredo intervened, standing between us before our fight could continue. "I get it. You two don't want to get along. But if we don't get past this scene, we can't move on, honey." He glanced at me, then Lucas. "Perhaps you two can compromise?"

Red flags went off in my head. That impetuous ass couldn't have found middle ground if he lived there. But if I wanted to get paid, what choice did I have?

It's for the kids, it's for the kids, it's for the kids.

I didn't look at Lucas as I nodded, somewhat in agreement.

"Fuck, can we just get this over with?" Lucas took his position in front of the mirror, ready to rehearse the routine. I joined him, and Alfredo counted us in.

A FEW DAYS PASSED, AND ALFREDO ATTEMPTED TO teach Lucas the more difficult moves of the routine, but he wasn't getting it. I wanted to step in and intervene a few times—blamed it on the teacher in me.

The night before we shot the scene finally arrived, and Alfredo must've been feeling the pressure because he stormed out of the dance room when Lucas missed a beat.

Alfredo had been on edge all day. It really wasn't fair to Lucas.

What the fuck? Did I actually pity the jerk? Maybe just a smidge.

"I'm not going to get it with him yelling at me like that," Lucas said, flustered.

I couldn't believe what I was about to do, but the guy looked completely hopeless. Dance wasn't his forte; I understood that much.

"Come here. We'll take it slow," I said.

He shot me a questioning expression, eyebrows wrinkled.

"Well? Come on. Let's get this over with so we can go

home." I held my pose as he walked up beside me. "On my count. Ready?" I stared at him in the reflection of the mirror, waiting for his response. His gaze met mine, and he nodded.

"One. Two. Three. Four."

I counted through the movements of the choreography, and though he fumbled a bit, he more or less started to get the steps down.

At one point, he went left instead of right and groaned. "This is impossible. Why can't I get this? It's been three days."

He was used to having everything come easily.

I took a breath before saying, "Lucas, some things take practice. Don't tell me you just picked up the guitar one day and knew how to play instantly."

He looked at me, his expression unreadable. "That's different. I love playing the guitar. I'm not passionate about dancing like you are."

Fair point. I kept a straight face, taking the starting pose once more. "One more time. We'll take a break after. If you get lost, focus on me."

He took a deep breath and nodded. We locked eyes.

That time we flowed through the movements smoothly—well, smooth enough for the five millionth time that night.

With all the dancing we were doing, he still managed to look fucking gorgeous as sweat glistened on his toned tattooed biceps. I retied my messy bun and huffed at my disheveled appearance.

He grabbed a white hand towel off the desk and wiped the perspiration from his brow. "You're a good teacher."

"Why do you sound surprised?"

"I'm not. I was trying to compliment you," he replied.

"Well, don't. I want you to get this dance down so this nightmare can come to an end." I grabbed my own towel from the duffel bag sitting next to the door. He'd hardly said a word to me these past few days we'd rehearsed, and suddenly he wanted to chat?

"You really don't like me, huh?" It sounded like he was standing right behind me, and I didn't have the courage to face him.

I didn't say anything, just continued to put my towel back in my bag.

"You don't even know me," he said.

Was that a tinge of hurt in his voice? No. It couldn't be. This guy could have whoever he wanted.

I turned to face him, taking in his sweet woodsy scent. God, I wanted to eat him up. Wait, no, I didn't. I wanted nothing to do with this man. "I know your type."

He crossed his arms, his stare bearing down on my soul. "And what is my type?"

I stepped back. "Late to everything, doesn't care about others, fucks anyone he can, has an issue with authority."

His lips formed a straight line. "First of all, being late was *not* my fault, and that Hard Rock incident was the first run-in I've had in years. And I haven't dated anyone in months."

Oh really? "That doesn't mean shit," I said, hugging my soft midsection. "Doesn't mean you haven't been fucking everyone else."

The corner of his mouth rose. "Why are you suddenly concerned about who I'm fucking?"

What an asshole. My nose flared. "You asked me to summarize your type."

"You have something against sex?" he asked.

Of course I didn't, but there was no way in hell I'd tell him that. My bottom lip slipped out from between my teeth. "That's none of your fucking business."

"When you bite your lip like that, it makes me think otherwise, Sunshine." He still had that roguish smirk on his stupid face.

What was it about him that made me want to fuck him and punch him at the same time?

"You're delusional. I'm gonna find Alfredo."

Being in that room alone with him was dangerous, because for some reason, I felt like I was walking on the knife's edge. With Lucas, I was becoming unpredictable.

W HEN I ARRIVED HOME FROM REHEARSAL THAT NIGHT, I fully intended to pick some random groupie's number from my contacts and invite her over. For some reason, I never hit the fucking call button. I couldn't even bring myself to send a goddamn text. Hell, I—Lucas Verduce—could have any pussy in NYC, but I hesitated. *Fuck.* Thinking about being inside some other chick made my dick limp. *What the fuck is happening to me?*

Damn. That spark in Julia's eyes and the way she bit that luscious bottom lip made my pulse increase and my dick twitch. She wanted me. Maybe she just wanted to fuck me, but that was progress compared to where we'd started.

I was such a sick fuck. That scowl on her beautiful face whenever I winked at her made my dick throb.

I couldn't fucking sleep thinking about Julia's hot anger and that sexy lingerie she'd worn for the lap dance scene. My dick begged for release. I reached beneath the sheet and stroked it. My breathing quickened with each lingering pass. I thought about Julia's breasts, her perky nipples peeking through the lacy material. I massaged my balls, sending waves of ecstasy through my body.

My pace increased when I imagined ripping her panties aside, watching my length slide up and down her pussy lips before thrusting into her warmth. *God, I want to fuck her until she screams, until she can't walk.*

Fuck, I was consumed by her scent, her smile, her presence. I wanted to slide my fingers up the front of her slender neck and stare into those passionate sparking eyes as I pumped into her.

My abs clenched. My free hand gripped the sheets. My eyes closed tightly, and the moment before that drink hit my face, her irate beauty was all I could see.

"Julia." Her name escaped my lips on a moan. I came all over my stomach.

Fucking hell, I need a shower now. Maybe I just needed to fuck her out of my system and that would resolve everything.

Why couldn't I be a normal guy and go after women who actually *liked* me for me? Women who wanted to be nice? Wanted to *love* me? Maybe I liked the challenge, or maybe I wasn't used to being rejected.

THE NEXT EVENING, ETHAN HAD SOME ERRANDS TO RUN. I decided to pick Julia up from her studio instead of meeting her on location.

The driver parked the SUV directly in front of the studio on the street. I took off my black sunglasses to get a better view of Julia. Through the tint of the wide window, I watched her interacting with one of her students. *Probably a private lesson.*

Julia smiled at the little brown-haired girl. She demonstrated some ballet move where she pointed her toe out and kicked high. The little girl followed suit, and Julia clapped in genuine excitement.

I didn't even realize I was smiling until I focused on my face mirrored in the car window. Through my reflection, she was beautiful. I could see the joy in her movements. Her long hair was styled in a neat bun, wisps of hair framing her delicate face.

It was obvious she loved her job, and in a way, I was envious. There was so much passion in the way she taught, so much encouragement in the way she smiled.

I envied the little girl.

The student left the studio with her guardian. After a few more minutes, Julia walked outside and opened the back passenger door to the SUV with her tote on her shoulder. She looked at me with a furrowed brow and tired gaze. The long nights were getting to her, and it was only the end of the first week.

"What're you doing here?"

"Get in, Sunshine." I slid my sunglasses over my eyes.

She glowered at me before climbing in and closing the door behind her. She said nothing else.

I hoped we'd run into traffic on the way to the shoot. It would be the perfect opportunity to try talking to her. I wanted to know more about her. What made her tick? *That isn't a crime. Right?*

My driver, Fred, knew to mind his own business even though we sat in silence in the bumper-to-bumper traffic. I sent a text to Ethan telling him we were going to be late. That didn't go over well with him considering he was the one to tell the lovely director the news.

Julia sat about a foot and a half away from me. Her left leg was crossed over her right, and she wore sexy ripped boyfriend jeans, green Converse, and a Nirvana tee. Her hair had been redone in one of those messy buns.

I couldn't help but grin, and she noticed.

Her eyebrows came together. "What?"

"Nothing. It's just . . ."

She looked about ready to fight me, as usual. "Just what?"

"You don't strike me as the typical ballerina," I said, knowing full well it would make her lose her shit. The corner of my mouth rose as I braced for her rebuttal.

Those dusty-pink lips thinned. "And what exactly is a typical ballerina to you?"

I shrugged.

"Please. Enlighten me," she prodded.

"Well, I've always pictured someone in pink wearing

those fluffy-ass tutus. Don't you all wear those leg warmers too?" I asked.

Her face flushed crimson with rage. "I don't need them in this weather, shithead."

"I've never seen a ballerina wear so much black." God, I knew I was asking for it. "And I'm the rock star here."

"Listen, asshole, I happen to like black and neutral colors. And for your information, I used to wear a lot of pink *and* white when I danced for a company," she said, still as pissed as ever.

"Did you quit because you couldn't wear black?"

She gritted out, "No. It was an injury."

Shit. She'd been injured? I didn't know that. Before I could stop myself, I asked, "How'd it happen?"

"How do all injuries happen?" Her glossy chestnut eyes bored into me. "An accident." She pursed her lips before turning her gaze out the window.

I could see from the closed-off look in her reflection that she was done talking to me. But I wasn't going to give up. I would get this girl and these feelings out of my system one way or another. *That's the plan, anyway.*

"You two have it down. All that's left is for you to sell it. Convince the world that you two are in love," Alfredo said as he shooed us toward the set.

"We'll make you proud, Alfredo," Julia said.

I nodded in agreement.

The setting was a huge circular fountain in the back of the mansion near the tennis courts and pool. Wardrobe fit me in a white tank, jeans, and black Converse. I was going to get soaked, so for me, makeup went quick.

I walked out onto the set as the sun made its final descent over the horizon. Lights illuminated the shallow blue waters. The band and their instruments stood inside the fountain, unplugged, obviously. I greeted Lita and the guys before making my way over to the director.

Julia padded up shortly after, wearing minimal makeup, her long hair down in all its natural wavy splendor. *She's beautiful.*

Before we jumped into the scene—or should I say the fountain—Katie said, "I know it's far-fetched, but you two need to act like you're in love and don't want to rip each other's throats out."

I draped my arm around Julia's shoulders. "Don't worry, boss. Julia and I are professionals."

Katie shot me a sidelong glare. "I know Julia is. It's *you* I worry about." Before she walked away, she added, "And what did I say about the *boss* crap?"

Julia made her way into the chilly fountain. Water splashed her. The white tank top clung to her slender curves, and the lines of the lacy bra and her hardened nipples made my dick stir.

"Stop staring. It's cold."

I smirked and leaned in. "I know."

She kicked water at me.

"Hey, cut that shit out," I warned, pointing my index finger at her.

As Katie walked back up to us, Julia splashed another wave at me, soaking us from the waist down.

"What the fuck are you two doing?" Katie exclaimed. "Great, just what we need—another fucking delay."

"Sorry, Katie," Julia said.

The director turned and hollered for the makeup team to bring towels while Julia flipped me the bird.

Julia practiced her movements while wardrobe dried me.

She's such a little fucking shit. Droplets of water rolled down her body as she twirled, kicking more water.

We did a few more takes. On the last one, we both tripped, and Julia landed straddling my enormous hard-on. Her eyes widened, and that spark flared in them like I'd done something wrong. I grinned as I held her hips and ground against her before helping her stand.

Katie stomped back over to us. "We're not fucking getting anywhere. We're running out of time. If you two don't get your shit together, we're gonna be here an extra day, and Mr. Jameson won't be happy about that. Unless you're gonna pay for it, Lucas?"

That wasn't the problem. *I really don't want to be in this fucking cold-ass water anymore.* No matter how much I wanted to continue to hold her wet body.

"We're taking a five-minute break, then we're gonna shoot it one last time," Katie added.

Julia and I stood outside of the fountain away from the crew, wrapped in heated towels. We really needed to get past this scene. I didn't want to piss off the producer this close to the end of our contract. *Fuck, I'm gonna have to play nice.*

"How can we work through this?" I asked.

"You can stop being an asshole."

I rolled my eyes. "Yeah, well, that's probably not gonna happen tonight."

She smirked, and that was the closest I'd come to getting that Julia smile.

"What can I do to get us past this fucking scene?" I stepped closer.

"I'm trying." Frustration dripped from her voice.

"Can you pretend you're teaching me for just a few minutes?" I asked, trying not to sound too desperate.

Her face seemed to soften. She nodded as the crew returned.

Katie cued the music, and we started our dance. Even though we'd practiced a hundred times, something was different this time. Our playful movements suggested we were in love. Julia was smiling—and at me no less. It was the smile she'd given her student earlier. My heart thrummed against my rib cage, and my lips curved, matching hers.

I was lost in our rhythm. The movements flowed freely between us. We were connected, eyes locked. Before I knew it, the music ended, our bodies coming together, ready for more. Her breasts pressed against me with each heaving breath.

"That's a wrap," Katie shouted, startling us. "About fucking time."

Lita jumped out from behind her keyboard. "Thank fuck. I need a drink." She walked toward the double doors of the mansion.

Julia's eyes met mine. It looked like she wanted to say something, but she just pulled away and headed for the pool house, where I assumed she had all her dry clothes. My dry clothes were probably in there too. I didn't think the crew wanted us tracking water into the mansion.

Kyle walked up in his equally soaked clothes and threw his arm over my shoulders. "I didn't know you could dance, man." He probably wouldn't ever let me live that down.

"I can't."

His eyes drifted over to Julia as she made her way to the pool house. "God, she's so fucking hot."

My blood started to boil. I didn't know why. It wasn't like I had any claim on her—not like I *wanted* a claim on her. But the thought of her fucking Kyle sent nausea roiling through my stomach.

"Those perfect tits, that beautiful mouth. I could do a lot with her." He smirked. "I bet I could bend her like a pretzel."

I'd heard enough. I shrugged his arm away and trudged over to the pool house in my wet Converse to change. He didn't say anything else after that. Probably just figured I was in one of my moods. Kyle walked toward Billy, who'd been splashing Mark in the fountain.

As expected, my dry clothes had been folded and placed in one of the bathrooms. Julia was in the other, and at the thought of her getting naked, my dick stiffened. I tried to push the image far from my mind as I changed into dry clothes and sneakers. I couldn't forget the way Julia and I had danced together. The way her body had moved with mine. The way she'd gazed into my eyes, like she truly was in love with me. In those moments, I hadn't known if I wanted these feelings for her.

Julia and I emerged from the pool house at the same time. Her hair was still damp, and she'd changed into the clothes she was wearing earlier. She padded away from me while putting her hair up in a bun. I couldn't help but notice the slight limp.

"Hey, you okay?" I fell into step with her.

She adjusted her heavy tote on her shoulder as she slowed her pace. "What do you want?"

I didn't let her annoyed look deter me. "You wanna go out with me and some of the crew tonight?"

"I can't. I have classes tomorrow," she said, her gaze fixed on the stone pavement.

"Yeah, but that's not until later in the day, right?"

She came to a halt and looked at me with a raised eyebrow. "How do you know that?"

"I saw your schedule in your office." I didn't want her to think I was a stalker. *Can't help that I have a photographic memory.*

She stared at me for a few seconds. "I suppose Mia could use another night out."

Fuck yeah. My heart skipped a beat at her response. It

wasn't much, but it was something. This was going to be a slow process. I wasn't used to pursuing women; they always pursued me. I had to stay on my fucking toes with Julia. She was one tough cookie.

I had the driver pick Mia up on the way to Nebula, which was more of a club than a bar. I trusted her to be my voice of reason, trusted her to keep me the *hell* off of Lucas. I'd used Mia as an excuse to come, but other than that, I didn't know why I'd agreed to it. Oh, wait. It was because my body wanted that fucking asshole. Lucas Verduce—rock star, musician, heartbreaker.

After I'd somewhat blindly signed the contract to dance in the music video, I googled him, though I didn't read all the articles thoroughly; I mostly paid attention to the headlines. The media ate up his love life.

Rock Star Lucas V. Walks Out of Victoria Secret Model's Penthouse.

Lucas Verduce Dates Movie Star Gracie Marquez.

Lead Singer Lucas Verduce Breaking Hearts . . . Again.

Lucas Verduce Breaks Up with Italian Supermodel.

And who knew what other women he'd dated in between that model and movie star. Yet despite his track record, I'd still said yes to going to the bar.

I'm definitely not staying focused.

Security escorted us to the loft area above the dance floor. The owner had that section reserved just for us.

Guess that's one of the perks of being associated with rock stars.

Thirty minutes later, the band and most of the crew members arrived at the lively bar. Strobe lights and loud music charged my senses.

Bodies crowded the floor below, gyrating to the beat of the thumping music. A few of the crew members took shots at one booth while others snuck away to dance.

Lucas sat in a booth by himself, sipping on amber liquid from a tumbler. A busty, leggy blond traipsed up and started talking to him. I wasn't sure what they were talking about, but her body language screamed, "I want to fuck you into tomorrow."

Gag me. I rolled my eyes and turned my attention to Mia, who was bobbing her head to the music. My leg was killing me. I shouldn't have pushed myself so hard in that last scene. These long nights were rough. I had to do something to get my mind off this pain.

"You wanna get a drink?" I asked her. Thankfully, the music wasn't blaring too loud in our little section of the club.

Mia looked cute in her yellow flower-print blouse, dark jeans, and ankle boots. Her hair was styled in an elegant bun. "Sure," she said.

I, on the other hand, was all grunged down in my ripped jeans, Nirvana tee, and green Converse. My hair was in a messy bun, strands of dark hair framing my face.

We reached the bar and waited for someone to take our drink orders. All the bartenders scrambled around making drinks for the patrons sitting at the bar.

Kyle, the band's rhythm guitarist, approached us. He leaned close and asked, "What're you ladies drinking tonight?"

Mia had a flirty smile on her face. "Whiskey sour."

His brow rose as if he was surprised—maybe even impressed—by her choice in drink, and then he looked at me.

"Crown and Coke," I said, and I received the same reaction from him. Had he really never met girls who didn't go for those fruity concoctions? Not that I had anything against them. I just preferred the taste of hard liquor. It all started when I'd snuck a shot of apple Crown from my dad's stash when I was around eighteen, and I was hooked.

Kyle signaled the bartender, and we had our drinks in hand before we knew it. We all returned to the exclusive lounge area. Lucas still hadn't moved from his booth. That blond was still there, along with a few others. I took a swig of my drink, and the dark liquid burned and bubbled down my throat. *Just what I need.*

We sat at another booth behind Lucas's. Mia and Kyle had sparked a conversation among themselves.

Great. I'm the fucking third wheel. I sipped my drink and people watched—mostly Mia shamelessly flirt with Kyle. I couldn't blame her. She was the type of girl who could do one-night stands, and I totally respected that. It just wasn't *my* thing.

I drank more as the evening went on, and Mia and Kyle did as well. They ended up on the dance floor together, leaving me alone in the booth. I decided to scroll through the messages on my phone. The theater manager had emailed me about the final payment again. I'd be getting paid from the production company in time to pay him.

A shadow fell over me as I clicked my screen off and stuffed it back into my front pocket. Before I realized it was Lucas, he'd scooted into my booth, making me slide against the mirror-paneled wall, trapping me.

"What the fuck?" I muttered, but he didn't hear me. "What're you doing?" I said louder.

He took a sip from his glass as dark hooded eyes met mine. Was that the same drink he'd had earlier? I looked to the table he'd been sitting at. The girls were preoccupied with Mark and Lita.

"What's it look like I'm doing?" he asked, testing me.

My blood warmed, pulse throbbing in my core beneath his intense gaze. I kept my face as neutral as possible. "Invading my space, as usual."

After another sip, he leaned in, the scent of top-shelf liquor on his breath. "Trust me, Sunshine. If I was invading your space, you'd know it."

I blinked a few times. Was he fucking flirting with me? The worst part was that my body responded. *Dirty bitch.* Apparently, my primal urges didn't care if the man was a fuckboy.

I placed my hand on his chest and pushed him away. "You're lucky we're in a public place."

He smirked. "I can make arrangements if you want."

I crinkled my nose. "In your dreams."

His gaze darkened as though he was confirming my last remark—that he actually dreamt about me, about us. I swallowed and looked anywhere but at him.

"I like your dad's band," he said, catching me off guard.

I looked at him with an incredulous expression and took a drink from my half-empty glass. "Yeah, right."

Mia and Kyle were still on the dance floor, gyrating to "Poker Face" by Lady Gaga. By the smile on her face, it looked like she was having fun.

Lucas slid his phone out of his jeans pocket, tapped the screen a few times, and showed me a playlist on his music app. Low and behold, at the top was "Lessons Learned" by In Your Head. At least he had good taste.

I pursed my lips before downing the rest of my Crown and Coke.

"He seems like a cool dude," Lucas said.

God, was he *really* trying to talk to me? I supposed I could be a decent human being and indulge him. I just didn't understand why he was wasting his time. There were other women in the club who actually *wanted* Lucas's attention.

"Thanks. He is," was all that came out of my mouth.

Aside from his flakiness, Dad was a great guy. He might have given me independence too early, but I'd learned to appreciate it through the years.

"Sometimes I wish my dad knew something about music. We'd actually have something in common," he said.

First of all, I didn't want to talk about our daddy issues in a noisy club. Second, if he wasn't going to leave me alone anytime soon, I was going to make this fun. "Fine. You want to talk? A shot for a question."

His brow rose. "Are you serious?"

Maybe he wouldn't be in the mood and sit somewhere else. Then again, who was I kidding? This man was fucking resilient.

"Dead serious. How many questions do you want?"

"Ten."

I frowned. "Five."

"Fine. I'll be right back." He stood, smoothing his dark Henley, which hugged his sculpted upper body in *all* the right places. "You're not gonna run away, are you, Sunshine?"

With a shrug, I folded my arms on the table. "Guess you'll just have to find out."

He walked away, but before he sauntered down the steps, he talked to one of his security guys and pointed at me. I assumed Lucas was telling the man not to let me leave.

"Asshole," I mouthed at both of them.

It was probably the liquor causing my blood to run hotter than usual, but I decided to blame it on Lucas. There was no way I could sneak past that big burly security guard.

I put the rim of the glass to my lips and realized I'd drunk it all.

Fuck. This wasn't my plan at all. I'd planned to have a

few drinks with Mia, go back to my apartment, and fall asleep to episodes of *Gossip Girl*, not play a drinking game with Lucas fucking Verduce. Why had I suggested it in the first place?

Oh yeah, because I'm fucking unpredictable around him. I groaned, hiding my face in my warm bare forearms.

In no time, Lucas came back with a tray of shots. He set it on the table and sat next to me, scooting in close. "So . . . a shot for a question?"

At least he'd ordered dark liquor. I nodded.

"You go first." He pushed the tray closer to me.

"I don't want to know anything about you," I said without thinking. "Nothing Google can't tell me, anyway." I wanted to swallow those words right after I'd said them. *Fuck. Did I just admit that?*

That familiar devilish smirk crept onto his full lips. "You googled me?"

Great. Because his ego needed more inflation. I inwardly palmed my forehead.

"That counts as a question." My lips curved up, and I handed him a shot.

"That's bullshit," he muttered before putting his lips to the rim and throwing it back. The man could handle his liquor. He didn't even cringe. That was when I knew I was royally fucked.

My alcohol tolerance was low, but I wasn't a quitter. I'd at least try to keep up.

"How old are you?" he asked, then took another shot.

At this rate, he'd be drunk in an hour—hopefully. Then

he'd leave me the fuck alone. Did I want that though? Of course I did. There was no time in my schedule for . . . whatever he wanted from me, which was probably just sex. Granted, the thought of fucking him wasn't a terrible idea. That was definitely the alcohol talking.

"Twenty-eight."

"Huh, you're two years older than me." He sat there, seeming to think of the next question, or maybe he was letting those last two shots marinate. "Why ballet?"

I shook my head. "I'm not answering that."

"Then you take a shot. It's only fair." He held up one of the small glasses.

With a regretful sigh, I took it from him and threw it back. The whiskey burned all the way down. I couldn't help but cringe. My eyes scanned the dance floor again, and Mia and Kyle were still moving their bodies to the music. They started making out. She was definitely getting laid tonight.

"You only have two more questions," I said, turning my attention back to Lucas.

He tossed another shot back like it was nothing, and the urge to punch him in his pretty rock star face was strong.

"Favorite sex position?" he asked.

Fuck. I grabbed another full shot glass and poured the contents down my throat. After swallowing, I pointed my index finger at him, leaning in close. "One more."

That stupid grin never left his face. His russet eyes met mine, and he inched even closer to me. His lips grazed my earlobe, lingering there for a moment before asking the last question. "On our next date, where do you wanna go?"

The palm of my hand met his shoulder, shoving him away. "You son of a bitch. This isn't a date." I pushed him out of the booth and stumbled, sliding off the seat. Those shots hit me hard as soon as I stood. I steadied myself, holding on to the table as Lucas stood next to me.

"Are you okay?" he asked, lips pursed in concern.

I looked through my lashes at him, butterflies fluttering in my stomach. It could've been the effects of the alcohol.

Mia ran up to me and grabbed my arm. Her pupils were dilated, cheeks red. She was fucking drunk. "Oh my god, Jules, look." She held up a small clear ramekin. "One of the crew members snuck in Jell-O tequila shots."

Before I could react, she shoved a lime wedge into my mouth, the green peel facing inward. She pushed me, and I stumbled, hitting the surface of the rectangular table, falling flat on my back. *What the fuck is going on?* My legs hung off the table as Mia lifted my tee, exposing my stomach. She flipped the ramekin upside down, sliding the cold wet Jell-O shot onto my skin.

She held me down. "You'll thank me later." A devious smile had taken the place of the sweet and innocent one she usually had.

"What?" I squeaked, spitting out the lime as my vision spun.

She grabbed Lucas's arm and pulled him in front of me. "What're you waiting for? Bon appétit," Mia said to him, shoving another slice into my mouth.

He gazed down at me, sprawled out on the table, and stepped closer. His dark eyes met mine as he lowered his mouth to the Jell-O shot on my belly, his warm breath tickling my skin. When I didn't protest, he sucked the shot into his mouth, but he didn't stop there. His tongue swirled and glided against me. In long languid strokes, he licked up any remnants of alcohol, leaving not a drop behind.

Fuck. My eyes fluttered shut as his warm tongue continued to work across my stomach. When I opened them, he leaned forward, pressing his firm body against me. His mouth hovered inches from my own.

The lime. The fucking lime. His lips brushed mine, along with the cold metal of his piercing. His teeth scraped against my lips as he bit into the lime. My hands gripped the blunt sides of the table, nails digging into the lacquered wood. He sucked all the juice out of the lime while it was still in my fucking mouth. A few drops of sour liquid trickled onto my tongue and down my throat. And fuck, he was hard. His length pressed firmly against my inner thigh. My legs betrayed me by spreading farther apart for him.

I realized a crowd of rowdy onlookers had gathered around me and Lucas. With all my strength, I pushed him off and straightened. The room spun, and Mia's smiling face was a blur.

Fuck. I grabbed my head, trying to will the floor to stop moving, but there was no denying it. I was going to throw up.

Without any notice, I stumbled away from the scene, covering my mouth, accidentally bumping people on the way to the bathroom. My other arm flailed women out of the way once I'd made it through the doors. I emptied the contents of my stomach into the toilet of the first accessible stall.

I'm never drinking again.

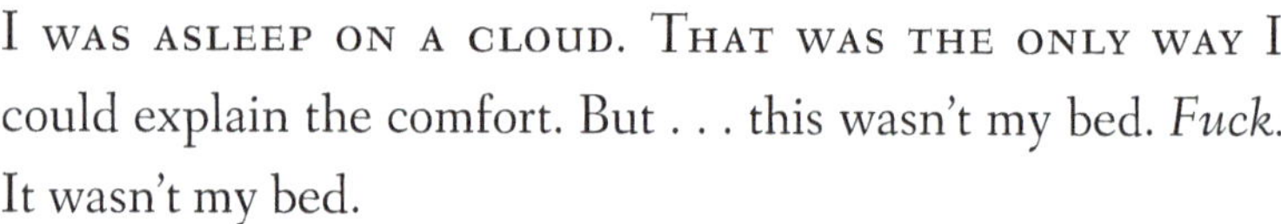

I WAS ASLEEP ON A CLOUD. THAT WAS THE ONLY WAY I could explain the comfort. But . . . this wasn't my bed. *Fuck.* It wasn't my bed.

My eyes shot open, and I took in the foreign surroundings. A beautiful panoramic view of the river and aesthetically pleasing buildings filled the large tinted window. There were black sitting chairs with modern lines next to that million-dollar view. A massive TV and entertainment center sat across from the huge bed I'd been sleeping in.

I blinked over to Lucas, who was sound asleep next to me, about a foot away. He wasn't wearing a shirt, and his jeans were unbuttoned and unzipped. The hard lines of his abs and chest were on full display.

He must work out a lot. With narrowed eyes, I leaned close, careful not to touch him. He was snoring softly. It was kind of cute.

His body shifted, and I held my breath, hoping he wouldn't wake up.

When he didn't, I swallowed and looked down at myself. I was in nothing but my pink panties and black padded push-up bra. *Where the fuck are my clothes?* I scanned the room more thoroughly, trying to stay calm. I was going to kill Mia.

My tote sat on one of the chairs in the room, along with my clothes, which were folded neatly.

I needed to get the fuck out of here.

It took focus for me to get out of bed without disturbing Lucas. I pulled on my jeans and tee, grabbed my bag, and attempted to find a way out of the maze of a penthouse.

My head throbbed as I tiptoed out of his room. I needed water. His open-concept kitchen was right next to the door of his room. I rummaged through the stainless-steel fridge and hit my elbow on the big door.

Clumsy bitch. I waited, hoping it hadn't woken him. Then I grabbed a bottled water and stared at the label. My eyes widened at the fact that he didn't drink the fancy shit. After taking a big gulp of the refreshing cold liquid, I wondered where my shoes could be. I found them in the walk-through closet on the way to the private elevator.

On my way through the modern abstract lobby, I hoped to God that I hadn't had sex with Lucas. I mean, I was pretty sure I would know. Right?

CHAPTER 11

Lucas

I SQUINTED THROUGH THE BEAMS OF SUNLIGHT HITTING my eyes and rubbed my face with my palms. Sitting up, I glanced at the empty space beside me. *Julia fucking left.* She hadn't even bothered to say goodbye—granted, I'd been asleep, but still. I'd washed her fucking clothes. If I hadn't, they still would've had vomit on them.

My dick stiffened at the thought of her lying in my bed in nothing but her bra and panties. I hadn't touched her. Not without her permission. I'd gotten a taste of her last night, and it had left me wanting more. If not for that fucking lime wedge, I would've slipped my tongue into her mouth. She probably tasted like sunshine and madness. *Fuck.* She ran to the bathroom and threw her guts up shortly after, which wasn't the reaction I usually got from women.

The penthouse was too quiet. I turned on the TV for some white noise while I fixed an espresso in the kitchen. The dark cabinets matched the color of Julia's onyx hair, while the sleek modern lines of the white marble were an elegant contrast to her honey-brown curves.

Ethan let himself into my place. He stood in the hall with his arms crossed, the buttons of his blazer undone. "Well, I heard last night was quite eventful."

I froze, glancing over at him as I stood in front of the stainless espresso machine. "I didn't get arrested." He *had* to appreciate that little fact.

He walked over and sat on a black barstool in front of the massive island. "Is it true you brought Julia back here?"

"Yeah, but nothing happened. I washed the vomit out of her clothes and let her sleep off the booze." When I turned to Ethan, he had that stupid smirk on his face again. "Don't fucking start with me, man."

"What? I didn't say shit." He held his palms up in defense. "It's just entertaining as fuck watching this chick break you down."

My eyebrows wrinkled. "She's not breaking down shit."

"Bro, you slept in the same bed *without* fucking her."

I sipped my espresso before saying, "You know I don't fuck drunk chicks."

He shrugged. "What about this morning?"

"She left before I woke up." I tried to keep the bitterness out of my voice.

Ethan didn't fucking know what he was talking about. Julia had been trashed, and I couldn't take advantage of her like that. Sober, she was intelligent and could see right through my bullshit. Drunk, she was a shit show. Hell, I didn't think I could ever take advantage of any woman.

"I'm done talking about this, fucker." I downed the espresso and walked into my room to get ready.

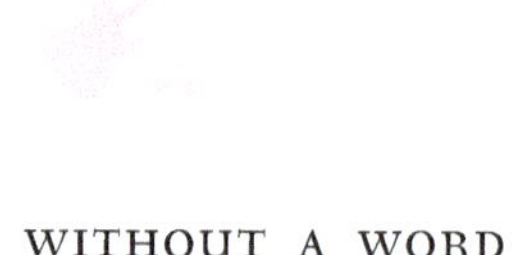

THE WEEKEND PASSED WITHOUT A WORD FROM JULIA, not that I'd expected her to fucking call me. Deep, deep, *deep* in my gut, I'd kind of hoped I'd hear something from her. *No such luck.* That following Monday, I attempted to talk to her, but we weren't in any scenes together.

Every time I tried to pull her aside to talk, Alfredo called her back to the dance room or Katie would call her over. Ethan had me so booked I didn't have time to pick her up at her studio all week. I couldn't help but feel there was some cosmic force keeping us apart. I didn't know why, but I *had* to make sure she was okay. I wanted to know why she'd left that morning. Granted, I had an idea.

I just wanted to talk to her more. Be near her. That night, next to her, was the best sleep I'd had in a long time.

Fuck. What's she doing to me?

I finally found time to pick her up on Friday. We ran into traffic as silence ensued between us. She sat next to me, looking out the window, her ankles crossed. She wore black leggings, Chucks, a black crop top, and a plaid shirt tied around her waist. Her hair was pulled back into a ponytail. *God, the things I could do with that.*

"Busy week?" I said, placing my hands in my lap.

She didn't look at me. "Yeah."

I wasn't one to beat around the bush. "Why'd you leave without saying anything last weekend?"

Julia still didn't face me as her shoulder rose, a tinge of annoyance in her voice. "I don't know. I didn't think it mattered."

"You could've stayed for breakfast or something." What the fuck was I saying? I didn't cook women breakfast; they cooked *me* food. I wanted to punch myself in the fucking face.

Those chestnut eyes studied me, and she bit her lip. I wanted to bite that lip, suck on it, lick it. I ran my tongue over my lip ring, resisting the urge. She swallowed, focused on my mouth for a moment.

"Cook? Didn't know you had any other skills besides music and fucking supermodels," she said, and I wanted to kiss her. I really was a sick fuck.

"Not many people know about my culinary prowess. I happen to make an outstanding omelet, Sunshine." I flashed her my trademark smile.

She uncrossed her ankles, still wearing that incredulous look on her face. "I'm sure."

"Can we just come to some kind of truce?" I asked. My patience was wearing thin this week. It always gave me a bit of fucking anxiety when a new song released. Would the fans like it? Would it attract new ones?

With an eye roll, she said, "As long as it has nothing to do with fucking you."

"Oh no, Sunshine. That's a perk." I grinned, and her cheeks flushed.

"Since we only have two more weeks to work together, I suppose I could be . . ." She sighed. "Less terrible." Another moment of silence passed before she said, "About that night. We didn't . . . you know?"

"Fuck?" I said, enjoying the look of embarrassment on her face. "No, Sunshine. You wouldn't be able to walk if we had." My voice was low and gravelly.

She stared at me with an unreadable expression. Why was it so difficult for me to get a read on this girl?

I cleared my throat. "Tell me more about your dad and his band. I really like their sound."

"Google them."

"Julia." I groaned, and it seemed to please her that she was getting under my fucking skin. "I'm trying to have a decent conversation with you."

The corner of her mouth rose as she shifted to face me again. "What do you wanna know?"

"When were they established?"

"I don't know the year, but I was fifteen when my dad put the band together."

"When did he start playing the drums?"

"He started at ten, but when he got my mom pregnant at eighteen, he quit to become an electrician. He picked it back up again when I was old enough to take care of myself," she said.

"What about your mom?"

She looked at her clasped hands in her lap and didn't say anything.

"Fuck," I whispered. "Did she die?" *Am I being insensitive?* How else was I supposed to ask that question?

Her brow furrowed, dark eyes meeting mine. "She might as well have. She left us when I was twelve."

I didn't know which was worse: death or abandonment. They were probably equally terrible in their own right. I wanted to wrap her in my arms and tell her I knew what it was like to lose your mother too soon. Instead, I muttered, "Shit. I'm sorry."

She seemed surprised by my response, and her beautiful features softened.

"My dad hasn't had time for me since my mom died. He's been obsessed with his career and making money. Like it could fill that hole," I said, gazing out the tinted window at nothing.

Her voice was small as she said, "I'm sorry about your mom."

"It was a long time ago." I shrugged off the empty feeling in my chest that urged me to change the subject. It was surprisingly easy to talk to Julia about these things. *I'm fucked.* "So, given your upbringing, what kind of music are you into?"

She fiddled her thumbs. "Depends on my mood."

"Do you ever listen to my band?" I asked out of pure curiosity.

"Honestly? No."

Her answer shouldn't have burst my bubble, but it did—fucking popped it like it was never there. "But you've at least heard of us, right?" God, why did I sound so desperate? *Get it together, Verduce.*

"I mean, I saw you on the news in cuffs. Does that count?" She smiled.

My heart turned to pudding. *Fuck, I want to be the cause of all her smiles.*

My own lips curved up. "I suppose so."

We spent the rest of the ride making small talk. She told me she had a major sweet tooth and loved red meat. I told her I was more of a health nut and loved the gym. She told me if she didn't love to dance, she would probably never exercise. I fucking loved the curves of her body and the confidence she exuded showing them off. That alone was sexy as fuck.

THE THIRD WEEK CAME ALONG, AND JULIA KEPT TO HER word, treating me "less terrible." But that wasn't to say we didn't fight, because we did. She managed to keep her insults to a minimum, and there were a couple instances where she could've said something but bit her tongue.

I was disappointed that the whole video shoot was coming to an end. Hanging out with Julia on our breaks had been the most fun I'd had in a while. The thought of us going our separate ways made me anxious, and I didn't know how to cope with that.

It was the final week of the video shoot, and that meant I wouldn't have to see or hear from Lucas Verduce ever again. The thought caused my heart to sink. Sure, we'd had a rough start, but after I'd agreed to be somewhat nice to him, working with him had become . . . tolerable, even pleasant.

Fuck. I can't develop any feelings for him, platonic or not. I didn't have time in my life for his bullshit.

The director saved the sex scene for the last day on set. I really should've read that fucking contract better. Granted, I wouldn't *really* be fucking him. It was acting. *I can do this.*

I sat in front of the vanity, my heart pounding at a quickening rate as the wardrobe girl picked out a lacy red bra with matching cheeky underwear and stilettos. *I might as well be naked.*

My makeup was light but not quite natural, and my hair had that "just fucked" tousle to it.

"God, you're so gorgeous, Julia. And lucky," the brown-haired makeup artist said as she finished touching up my face.

Sure as hell didn't feel lucky—the opposite, in fact. I was not looking forward to being in a room of about a dozen people watching me fake sexing Lucas Verduce. I clenched my hands into fists in my lap.

"Julia, you okay?" Ethan walked into the dressing room as I stood and shrugged into a white terry cloth robe.

I peered at him through the reflection of the mirror and breathed. "Yeah. Fine. Why?"

"You look nervous. Want a shot of whiskey to take the edge off?" He had an amused expression on his handsome face. I didn't know Ethan all that well, but he seemed like a nice guy. From what I could tell, he had Lucas's best interests at heart.

"No, I'm fine." Alcohol was the last thing I needed. "Thank you though."

"They're ready for you in there."

Ethan led me to one of the many large bedrooms in the mansion. They'd chosen one with a row of floor-to-ceiling windows. The sun shone into the room perfectly.

Lucas lay on the already-messy bed in nothing but red boxers. I gazed at the hard lines of his stomach and the sculpted V that disappeared beneath the waistband of his briefs. A warmth erupted between my legs, working its way through my entire body.

Traitor. I chewed on my bottom lip, noticing the slight

bulge in his boxers. God, was he semihard already? *Fuck me.* Technically, he was about to.

"Like what you see, Sunshine?" He grinned.

Couldn't blame him for his self-confidence. I liked his body, and against my better judgment, he'd been steadily wearing me down. I despised him for it. My eyes narrowed as I tore my gaze from him.

Katie walked on set and said, "We're gonna play this scene by ear. But do *not* remove any other clothing, Lucas. You can take off her robe, but that's it. We're not filming a fucking porno."

"Yes, ma'am," he said with a two-fingered salute.

She walked away, grumbling something inaudible.

"We're going to film some shots from far away first," Katie said.

"Let's get this over with." I let out a huff and climbed onto the bed as the instrumental for "My Crimson Love" filled the room. He wasted no time in untying my bathrobe and sliding it off my shoulders.

I straddled his lap, keeping my crotch inches from his. With my back facing the camera, I bit out, "You better fucking behave."

He sat up, and his hands glided up my bare waist and down to my thighs. Then he worked them around to my ass cheeks and gave them a firm squeeze.

I gasped, inwardly cursing my body's response.

He nuzzled against my collarbone and said, "Should've known you like the top."

Katie interrupted through the music, "Okay. We're going to get Lucas lip-synching now."

I remarked, "Thank God. I'd be completely turned off if you talked this much during *real* sex."

His dark eyes bored into mine as the lyrics started, and he whispered them to me. "Our love is reckless, our love is insane, our love is tough, and morally gray, but it's mine, my crimson love."

"We're going to pan in on Julia's face now," Katie said.

"Why don't you fuck me and find out?" Lucas's soft lips grazed the shell of my ear.

His breath sent a chill down my spine, and my pussy fluttered at the sensation. He played my traitorous body like the strings of his guitar as my brain struggled not to give in to his mind games. My nostrils flared, and I bit down on my lip, trying not to lose myself in the pleasure of his touch.

"Julia, I know it's difficult, but could you at least look like you're enjoying this?" Katie said. "Lucas, I want you on top now."

Fuck. He had me on my back in the next instant. His hands drifted up my shins to my thighs and stopped at my lace-clad breasts. He massaged and squeezed them as his mouth caressed my stomach, sending tingles to the warmth between my legs.

I decided to take the upper hand and flip him onto his back, running my hands up his lean stomach and pecs, feeling his muscles tense beneath my fingertips. His eyes drifted closed. I grinned and continued gliding my lips up to his collarbone. He flinched when my tongue flicked against the taut skin there.

"If you keep doing that, I'm going to fuck you for real," he gritted out.

"No talking, remember?" I straddled his hips and settled myself on his long hard length.

"Fuck," he seethed, gripping my hips and helping me grind against him.

"Exaggerate your hip movements more, Julia," Katie said.

That's exactly what I did, and the torture was apparent on his face. My slow, hard motions caused him to grit his teeth, and I relished every moment. His nails dug into the backs of my thighs, and I winced at the fleeting pain. Bunching my hair up to air off the back of my neck, I continued to ride him.

His dark gaze met mine once more, pupils dilated, filled with lust. I couldn't help but grin. Then he thrust his hips into mine, and a small sigh escaped me.

He rolled me onto my back again and worked himself against my damp pussy. Leaning on his forearms, he whispered, "You were so close to making me fucking come. Are you proud of yourself?"

I grinned. "Actually, yes." Who knew I could humble a rock star by simply dry humping him? Not that I'd be doing *that* again anytime soon.

"Okay, we're going to take a few close-up shots," Katie said.

I'd almost forgotten there were people in the room.

A few hours passed of take after take of me and Lucas essentially getting each other off before Katie finally called, "That's a wrap! Good job, everyone!"

I grabbed my robe, shrugged it on, and headed to the dressing room, satiating my urge to get the fuck out of there before my body betrayed me again. Should I have felt guilty for leaving Lucas Verduce with a massive hard-on? Probably, but I was sure he had groupies who could easily take care of that problem.

That was possibly the most intense scene of this whole video shoot. I gazed at myself in the mirror of the portable vanity, hands trembling as I removed the makeup from my face with a wipe. My hair was messier than before, and the dark strands sticking out in random places implied I'd been thoroughly fucked. But the pulse in my pussy said otherwise.

Fuck. It had been a while since I'd had sex. I typically didn't do one-night stands, but every once in a while, when my alter ego took over, I made a few exceptions. Could I make an exception for Lucas? All he wanted was sex, right?

No. What the hell am I thinking? We were like fire and ice. If not for the video shoot, we probably wouldn't ever get along.

I huffed, needing some kind of release or distraction.

AFTER CHANGING INTO DENIM SHORTS, A BLACK TANK, and flip-flops, I threw my hair up into a loose bun and headed out to the pool where everyone had congregated. A few crew members had jumped into the glistening water. I didn't blame them. My skin warmed from the sun's rays, causing perspiration to form on my brow.

The rest of the workday turned into a party. A DJ had set up next to the pool house and was blasting some techno remix, and an open bar on the other side of the rectangular pool served beer and other mixed drinks. I grabbed a bottled water and watched as everyone socialized.

Katie walked up to me, a martini glass in hand. "Hey, Julia. You did great in there. You've been so poised and professional to work with compared to other women they've paired with Lucas."

I really didn't think that much of it, especially after that last scene where I bit his shoulder to get a reaction from him. I'd also accidentally left teeth marks in his skin. *Whoops.*

"I . . . was just doing what I was hired for."

"I wish there were more girls like you, Julia Blackwell." She pulled me in for a short hug. "You don't let emotions get in the way of your work."

I wasn't sure if that was a compliment. I didn't have time to return the hug before she pulled away. "Thanks, I think."

"Well, enjoy the party. You deserve it." With that, she padded away, steadily making her way around the poolside.

I should've probably left after that, but I didn't. As I took a swig of my water, Lucas made his way up in jeans, a fitted white tee, and black Chucks. Why couldn't he wear not-so-distracting clothes? Then again, he'd probably look good in a trash bag. *Shit.*

"What?" I crossed my arms upon his approach, still holding my bottled water. "The shoot is over, so don't feel obligated to talk to me anymore."

His eyes roamed the length of my body as he pushed his black-framed sunglasses up the bridge of his nose. "We're back to this? What happened to treating me 'less terrible'?"

"That agreement is now void." I poked his muscled chest.

He chuckled and grabbed my hand, pulling me into him. I didn't falter at his sudden closeness.

"You have no fucking idea how crazy you make me." His voice dropped an octave.

I didn't step back, but that didn't mean I wasn't a little afraid. I rolled my eyes. "That's not my problem."

His finger reached beneath my chin, forcing me to look at him as he leaned close, our lips an inch from touching. "If you roll your eyes at me one more time, Sunshine, I swear—"

My jaw clenched before I taunted, "You'll what? You're not gonna do shit. Not with all these people around." I gestured to the pool area.

The corner of his mouth rose, and I instantly regretted saying those words to him. In the next moment, he lifted my petite frame over his shoulder. I struggled against him, but it was no use. He was too fucking strong. He walked over to the edge of the pool. Before I could get words out, he jumped into the deep end with me on his shoulder.

Holy shit! The water was cold but refreshing, and fuck, I still had my phone in my pocket. I burst through the surface of chlorinated liquid and swam toward the shallow end of the pool. Lucas was still treading at the other end, laughing at my demise.

My nostrils flared, eyes narrowing. "You think this is fucking funny, asshole? I still had my phone on me." I raised my dripping cell, which had all my student contacts and parent info. There hadn't been a reason for me to get a business phone. *Until now.* I hadn't thought anything like this would ever happen. Should've known better.

"You better hope it still works," I said before walking up the corner steps of the pool and making my way to the pool house.

Luckily, the bathrooms were equipped with those spin dryer contraptions, so I started stripping. It didn't take long for Lucas to walk into the large square room, which had only one toilet, a shower, and a pedestal sink. I really wasn't in the mood for more of his shit.

He caught me in my sports bra, shorts unbuttoned and unzipped, showing off my black cotton panties. My hair was down, still drenched. I was pretty sure I looked like shit, not to mention I was still fuming about my phone.

I spun around and leaned against the porcelain sink. "What the fuck do you want? Haven't you done enough damage?"

He locked the door, and my heart sank into my stomach. After he peeled off his shirt and threw it on the floor, he just stood there, staring at me. His eyes went to my phone, which I'd set on the sink.

"I'll pay for a replacement."

"I don't *want* you to pay for a replacement."

A muscle ticked in his jaw. "But I *want* to."

"I won't let you." My arms were crossed over my chest, and I made sure to keep my distance from him.

He ran a hand through his wet hair. "I'm buying you another fucking phone, and you're gonna take it."

"No, I won't," I said in my calmest voice. "I'll just send it back."

His body closed in on me before I could react. He snaked his arm around my waist, pulling me against his hard body. I braced my hands against his tattooed chest while his other hand sank into my wet hair. He tugged my head back, giving himself full access to my throat.

A mixture of chlorine and his cedar-and-vanilla scent filled my nostrils. I couldn't help but whimper.

"What're you doing?" I knew it was a stupid question, but I had to be sure this wasn't a dream. My mind played tug-of-war with my body once again.

He let go of my hair and placed his index finger to my lips. "Stop fighting this." His hand slid to one of my breasts and squeezed, drawing a strangled noise from me.

Fuck, why does his touch have to feel so good?

He reached beneath the band of my bra and ran his thumb over my pebbled nipple, sending a jolt of pleasure throughout my entire body. When he pinched it, I arched into him with a gasp. I had to remind myself he'd done this with plenty of women, and that was why he was so good.

"You have no fucking idea how hard it is to be around you," he rasped.

The corner of my mouth rose. "I can leave if you want."

He tightened his hold on me. "Don't even fucking think about it."

When his hand moved from my breast to my ass, I released a breathy moan and bit down on his shoulder. His chest rumbled in approval, soft breaths caressing my neck.

Fuck, I liked his roughness way too much, and if I gave in, he'd probably leave me alone. God knew my pussy ached for his dick. I reached down and rubbed his length through his wet jeans as my other hand wrapped around his nape, pulling his mouth to mine. He caressed my lips as though he craved me, *needed* me.

He lifted and set me on the edge of the sink. "Fuck. These lips." He ravaged my mouth. "This skin." He brushed his lips along the side of my neck and bit down at the base. I let out a strangled noise as he pulled my hips against his.

"No talking." My teeth grazed his collarbone.

He growled, setting my feet on the floor before pulling my shorts and underwear off. Then he kissed me, pushing me up against the white wall tiles. My gaze traveled down as he lowered his jeans, and his dick sprang toward me. He had a condom on in no time.

Fuck. Was this really happening?

He lifted me from the backs of my thighs, and his tip parted my pussy lips. As he slid inside me, he let out a grunt and hissed, "Fuck, so warm."

My mouth parted, letting out a breath at the fullness of him. "You said you could fuck me 'til I couldn't walk," I whispered in his ear. "Prove it."

His chest vibrated, and without another word, he pulled

out. I whimpered at the loss. Then he buried his dick deep inside my pussy, digging his nails into my thighs.

This has to be a sin.

In the mirror across from us, I made out the hard lines of his back, his strong broad shoulders, and how his firm ass contracted as he thrust into me hard. His vigorous movements rattled the pictures hanging on the wall.

Breaths ragged, I bucked my hips, driving him even deeper into me, hitting *that* spot over and over. *Fuck.* He was going to make me come. His pace quickened, and I could tell he was nearing his own release.

"Goddammit, you feel so fucking good," he murmured against my neck.

I moaned. "Fuck, yeah. Don't stop." I was incapable of putting together coherent sentences.

"Come for me, Sunshine." He fucking bit my shoulder and I squealed, the pain pushing me even closer to my impending climax.

"Fuck," I whispered. "So close." With a few hard thrusts, I shuddered, and a wave of pure ecstasy flowed through me as my walls pulsed around his length. Not a moment later, his stomach clenched, and he pushed into me one last time. His dick throbbed inside me, my pussy still contracting. A sultry groan fell from his lips.

He kissed me one last time, then rested his head on my shoulder as we caught our breath.

Once I came down from that mind-blowing orgasm, I shimmied down his body, gathered my wet shorts from the floor, and threw them into the spin dryer.

Definitely have to count this one.

He leaned against the wall for another second or two before he discarded the condom and pulled up his wet jeans.

My shorts, tank, and underwear weren't completely dry, but they'd do for the ride home. As I dressed, he put his shirt into the spin dryer and stared at me. "I want you to come to our concert this weekend at the Beacon Theatre."

I pocketed my phone. "I don't know. I have a lot to do before the recital."

He wrapped his arm around my waist and pulled me close. Cupping his free hand around my nape, he caressed my mouth before murmuring against my lips, "I really want you there."

God, this man had me melting into him. What the fuck was happening?

Stay focused. You don't have time for this.

I backed away from him. "I'll think about it." Before I walked out, my lips curved up. "Oh yeah, and Lucas?" I met his dark hooded gaze. "I can walk just fine."

His lips formed a straight line.

I winked at him before traipsing out of the bathroom and on with my life.

It had been seven fucking days since the last time I saw her. Her fragrant flowery scent and that dark, often-messy hair haunted my senses. Her sweet, salty smooth skin and, goddammit, that fucking smile. The way she moaned and moved her hips while I pounded into her in the pool house bathroom. Fuck me, I wanted more. I wasn't supposed to want more. It was *supposed* to be a one-and-done sexcapade. *Dammit.*

I sat on the edge of the wooden stage of the Beacon Theatre with my guitar, fiddling with some chords and lyrics. There was a song in there somewhere; I just had to find it. We were on a thirty-minute lunch break, and while everyone left to go eat, I'd opted to stay. I needed some time to myself.

The week had been a shit show with the release of the music video. We had parties to make appearances at and interviews to attend. On top of that, we needed to rehearse.

The video had really taken off, hitting over a million views on the web in the first day. It had been a long time since one of our songs had hit like that, but for some reason, it just didn't matter as much to me.

"Okay. What's wrong?"

I peered up at Ethan's concerned mug and frowned. "The fuck you talking about?"

He unbuttoned his black blazer and sat next to me on the stage. "I'm talking about you doing the bare minimum in your interviews. Leaving events and parties at midnight. Skipping out on pussy."

I had fully intended on resuming with my usual habits: music, alcohol, and pussy, though not in that particular order. But Julia had fucked up all my plans. All I could think about was her, and it was driving me mad, to the point where I'd started writing lyrics again. *Fuck.* Did this mean she was my muse?

"I don't know, man. I'm over it." My right hand continued to strum the black Fender guitar while my other one worked the strings against the frets.

"I know what's going on here," Ethan said, leaning away from me.

"The fuck you do. I just want to get this concert over with and work on some new music."

He let out a breath. "That's gonna have to wait, bro."

I stopped playing and gazed at him. "Fuck. Another tour?"

"An East Coast tour, US only." When I didn't respond, he said, "What did you expect with this spike in sales?"

I shrugged. "I don't fucking know. That they'd take their money and leave us the fuck alone. Do the others know?"

He shook his head. "Not yet, but I'm pretty fucking sure they'll all be stoked."

Dammit. I didn't want to go on this tour, but it would probably be the last one before our contract expired. "I want Julia on the tour." It came out like word vomit.

A knowing grin crept onto Ethan's face. "Is *the* Lucas Verduce fucking lovesick?"

"Fuck you. It'll be good for publicity, especially after that last article about me. And the fans seem to love her. Have you read the comments?"

He stared at me with that incredulous smirk. "I can't believe you're saying this right now. So, let me get this straight. You wanna contract Julia as what? A dancer? Fake girlfriend? What?"

Now he was just being a smart-ass. I rolled my eyes. "Hire her on as a dancer."

He crossed his arms. "Okay. But there's no guarantee she'll agree to sign another contract with us. She got what she wanted."

"Come on, chicks always want more. I'll talk to her if I have to." My hand continued to strum the strings of the guitar, making a lovely melodic sound.

"What about Mia?" he asked.

My brow rose. "What *about* Mia?"

"Julia's gonna want her to go." He looked down at his clasped hands.

I narrowed my eyes. "Do you have a thing for Julia's best friend?"

It had been a while since Ethan had been interested in someone. He wasn't as bad as me or Kyle, but he definitely had his moments. After he had his heart broken by his high school sweetheart, his career always took precedence over everything. With the exception of his parents, sister, and niece.

He let out a sarcastic laugh and got to his feet. "Don't be ridiculous. Do you know if Julia's coming tonight?"

"I don't know. Her fucking phone fell in the pool, remember? Were you able to send her a new one?"

"She said she doesn't need it."

"What do you mean, she doesn't need it?" I asked. Should've known she'd refuse it. I had half a mind to deliver the new phone to her myself.

"She said her phone's fine." Ethan shrugged. He had that fucking smile on his face. "Whose fault was it, by the way?" His hands fell to his hips. "You know, some of the crew members saw you follow Julia into the pool house bathroom. What do you have to say for yourself?"

A corner of my mouth rose. I couldn't lie to him about it. Then again, I wouldn't admit it either. "Just get ahold of her and ask if she'll be attending tonight. Make all the arrangements for her."

"Fine," he drawled. "But don't get mad at me if she says no."

"If that happens, let me know. I'll change her mind." I

placed my guitar aside and stood, stuffing my hands into my jeans pockets.

Ethan chuckled. "In the four weeks I've gotten to know her, I highly doubt that."

The other band members started trickling in.

"Would you go? There isn't much time." I grabbed my guitar again.

As much as I hated to admit it, Ethan was right. There was probably nothing I could do or say to make Julia attend our concert tonight. She did things on her own terms for her own reasons, and I admired her for that. But that didn't mean I wasn't going to try.

Whether she wanted to admit it or not, we'd formed some kind of relationship the last three weeks of shooting. It might have been a shallow one, but I wanted to change that. I wanted to know every dirty little detail of her life. It was stupid of me to think I could fuck her one time and be done.

That last fucking comment tormented me. *I can walk just fine.* She didn't know it, but I was going to get her back for that. I'd never received any complaints before Julia. Despite her completely hating my guts, I enjoyed her company more. She never came off as fake, and I loved that she wasn't pining for my attention.

Fuck. I didn't want to admit it—not to myself, not to Ethan, and most definitely not to my bandmates. I wasn't going to admit that I—Lucas Verduce—was falling for Julia fucking Blackwell.

T*HANK FUCKING* G*OD.* A*LL* I *HAD TO DO WAS PUT MY* phone in rice, and it started right up the next day. Ethan tried to send me a new one, but I'd sent it back with a note that mine still worked. There was no way in hell I was taking any handouts.

Stupid Lucas Verduce. Sure, he'd made my legs shake as I came and sent shivers down my spine with his rough tantalizing touch, but something inside me still wanted to loathe him. *I can't get involved with him.*

No Blood, No Alibi's concert was tonight. I hadn't even told Mia about any of it. She was going to freak the fuck out, and I didn't feel like dealing with her Mia-ness. But I *had* to tell her.

I sat behind the reception desk, fiddling with a pen, attempting to keep my mind busy with financial reports.

Mia traded a glance with me as she swept the floor.

"So . . . you despising Lucas doesn't mean I have to stop seeing Kyle, right?"

What the hell was she thinking? Didn't she know anything about these rock star types? I let out a breath. "You're seriously going to keep seeing him?"

She nodded. "Yeah, why not?"

I studied her. "Oh, I don't know. Maybe because you just went through a breakup. And haven't you seen the news? Kyle and Lucas are both allergic to commitment."

"Yeah, but you can't believe everything you read on social media or the media in general." She met my gaze. "I don't know, Jules. I *really* like him."

Mia was stubborn, like me. I knew anything I had to say about the matter would only go through one ear and out the other. The only thing I could do in this instance was accept and support her feelings. "Just promise me you'll be careful."

She huffed. "Yes, Mom. I promise you have nothing to worry about." She stared at me for a second. "So, what about Lucas?"

"What *about* Lucas?" I rummaged through the papers on the desk.

"You haven't said a word about anything after the last day of the shoot," she said. "Something must've happened."

My mouth clamped shut.

Her eyes widened. "Something happened, didn't it?"

Oh no. I couldn't withhold the truth from her any longer. It was coming out like verbal diarrhea. I walked out from behind the desk. "Fine, yes. I had sex with him, okay?"

Mia dropped the broom as an ear-piercing squeal

escaped her. She rushed up to me with the biggest smile on her face, like I'd discovered hidden treasure or some shit. "Bitch, you fucked a rock star! You're my hero."

My lips twitched. I was taken aback by her dramatic reaction. I should've prepared myself better for her high-pitched screams. "Fuck, Mia, your nails." I winced, freeing myself from her grasp. "And it's not a big deal."

She gazed at me with her big brown eyes, suspicion clear on her face. "You say that a lot when it comes to him." She placed her hands on her hips. "Why is that?"

If she wanted me to admit that I'd formed a modicum of feeling for that fuckboy, she would be disappointed. "Because it's true. Seriously, Mia. Is his title and money all you see when you look at him?"

Her eyebrow rose. "Uh, no. I also see a sex god. Honestly, what're you so afraid of? That he actually might like you?"

"Highly unlikely. I've been the biggest pain in the ass I can be to him." My phone vibrated on the desk.

Mia peered over to read the screen. "Why is Ethan calling you?"

I let out a sharp breath. "He's been calling me all day."

She cocked a brow. "What's he want?"

I shrugged, knowing exactly what he wanted.

That dreaded devilish smirk crept onto her face. Before I could react, she snatched my phone from the counter and answered it. She was so fucking fast, or maybe I was that slow. "Bitch."

She walked away. "Hey, Ethan. No, it's Mia. Julia is

busy at the moment. Concert? At the Beacon Theatre? Yeah, we'd be happy to attend."

I was going to murder her. I ran my palms down my face.

She smiled sweetly at me. "Yeah, we'll be ready by then. Great. Bye."

"Mia, what did you fucking do?" I gritted out, my pulse pounding in my ears. I took a deep, calming breath.

Her eyes widened at my irate response. "Jules, it's just a concert. Look, we're gonna go to the concert and have a nice girls' night. You don't even have to talk to Lucas if you don't want to. We can sneak out before their last set."

"What about Kyle?" I crossed my arms. "You actually gonna keep it in your pants tonight?"

"For you, yes." Her smile faded. "I know this is crazy scary, that someone might actually want a future with you, but you really need to stop thinking of what you could lose. Start thinking of what there is to gain."

Easy for her to say. She'd never been abandoned by anyone—not voluntarily, anyway. I remembered that day like it was yesterday. Mom looked me in my eyes and didn't bat an eyelash as she pulled out of our driveway. The emptiness of not having her in my life tortured me *every* fucking day. Then my dad had started to slowly become less involved in my teenage life.

I blinked back tears, staring at Mia. She'd triggered something in me, hit a nerve. I felt like I was drowning in the dark ocean waters, being pulled deeper and deeper into the place I'd worked hard to forget about.

With a short breath, I rolled my shoulders back and

padded into my office. "Finish cleaning. I have some paperwork to do before we go."

MIA AND I MADE OUR WAY BACK TO MY APARTMENT after we locked up the studio. She hopped into the shower as I stood in my small walk-in closet, picking my outfit. I opted for a loose black AC/DC tee, ripped jeans, military-style boots, and a plaid shirt tied around my waist. I styled my hair in a ponytail and put on a faded gray trucker hat.

Mia walked out of the bathroom wrapped in a white towel. She scanned my outfit and shook her head as she walked past me. There was no use in her giving me advice about how I should dress. Through the years, she'd just learned to accept me as me. I appreciated her for that.

"It's a good thing I left some of my clothes here." She rummaged through the clothes hanging on the dowel.

"Is that why you buy me clothes, so you can wear them later?" I couldn't help but grin in amusement.

"Essentially." She flashed her pearly whites.

I decided to turn on the TV for some white noise while Mia got ready. Flipping through the channels, I came across *E! News*, and there *he* was in all of his tattooed glory.

Will I never be free of this man?

"Congratulations on the success of No Blood, No Alibi's music video. The fans seem to adore the love interest," said the dark-haired anchorwoman.

Lucas's usual messy hair was slicked back, and he wore a black suit that hugged him in all the right places.

"For fuck's sake," I whispered, hating my body's visceral response to him. Hating myself for wanting more of him.

"What's next for you guys?" the woman asked.

Lucas sat in a chair across from the interviewer. The background was black, and the band's logo hung on the wall behind him. "We're going on an East Coast tour to promote the new song."

"There are rumors that you've been seeing the woman who played your love interest in the music video. Can you confirm?"

My cheeks warmed.

Lucas shot her that charming fuckboy smile, and his dark eyes gazed into the camera as he said, "No comment."

I'd seen enough and turned off the TV. What was he implying there? I shouldn't have cared because our little moment in the bathroom was a one-time thing.

It didn't take long for Mia to throw on a sheer white tee, torn blue jeans, and black platforms. She styled her long dark hair in waves and did her makeup last. I'd already put some eyeliner and lip balm on. That was usually the extent of my beauty routine.

We headed out the door just in time and scurried down the stairs and through the lobby. A tinted SUV was waiting next to the curb on the street. I recognized the driver, Fred. He was a cool guy.

I started to bounce my knee as we neared the venue but had no idea why I was so nervous. We planned to leave before they finished their last set, so it wasn't like I was going to talk to him at all. The success of his music video probably kept him super busy.

When we arrived, the cool spring breeze hit my cheeks as we climbed out of the car. People lined the outside of the building, wrapping around to the parking lot. Mia and I started toward the back of the line.

"Julia! Mia!" Ethan rushed up to us. "Where are you going? We have seats reserved for you two. Come on." He led us inside past the podium and the six bouncers manning it. Mia and I definitely got some dirty looks from the women in line. A few of them recognized me from the music video. *Great. Just fucking great.*

We entered the dimly lit building and continued up some steps to the upper level, where men in dark suits stood monitoring the people there.

"This is the VIP area. I gotta go backstage, but enjoy the show." Ethan walked away, leaving us standing at the railing of the loft. I'd never been inside the Beacon. The designs in the ceiling were intricate and detailed with gold accents. It gave me *The Great Gatsby* vibes.

Mia and I had a clear view of the stage. The band and stage crew were doing last-minute checks on the equipment as music played in the background. A large crowd filled the space below, and I was pretty sure everyone in the audience had an alcoholic drink in their hands, except me. I wouldn't make *that* mistake again.

The stage lights brightened as the seating area darkened, and the MC announced all the members of the band. Lucas was announced last, and he walked onstage in all his charismatic splendor. My insides warmed at the sight of him. I scowled at the tingling sensation in my stomach.

"What's that face for?" Mia looked at me, amusement on her features.

"He's just so—"

"Hot, talented, sexy, irresistible?" Mia teased.

I rolled my eyes. "How about arrogant, obnoxious, and insufferable?"

She shook her head and threw her arms into the air, giving up on me.

She did have a point. He looked exceptionally hot in his distressed black jeans, which clung to his toned thighs. He wore a fitted white tee, a silver thumb ring, and a black rope necklace with some kind of small emblem I couldn't make out. His dark hair was tousled in its usual "just fucked" manner, and I couldn't help but remember how he'd felt inside me. *Shit*.

No Blood, No Alibi began their first set. Mia and I danced to the rhythm of the music as Lucas sang his heart out. His and Kyle's riffs on their guitars blew my mind. Billy had his moments on the drums, and I was pretty sure Lita made me come a little the way she glided her fingers across that keyboard.

At the end of that set, the band walked off the stage. A short intermission began, and I hoped to God Lucas wouldn't try to find me.

I swallowed as nausea rolled through me, and my

breathing accelerated. I clutched my chest as though that would stop it from constricting.

Mia seemed to notice. "Hey, what's wrong?"

"I'm not ready to face him tonight," I shouted through the loud filler music.

"You wanna leave?" Mia asked, grabbing both my hands.

My stomach churned, and I realized I hadn't eaten anything. It was stupid, but I didn't want to risk seeing Lucas before I was ready. The question was, when would I ever be ready? *Why the fuck did I agree to this in the first place?*

My pulse raced as we hurried for the staircase of the loft and made our way through the crowd. A leggy blond woman stopped me in the lobby, grabbing my forearm. She looked familiar. I thought she was one of the women talking to Lucas the night I'd gotten shit-faced.

"Hey, you're the girl from the music video." She smiled at me in her hot-pink form-fitting dress and matching stilettos. "They really downgraded." She looked me up and down. "Compared to the other women in his other music videos."

My eyes narrowed. "The other music videos didn't make number one on the charts."

Mia intervened. "Who the fuck are you, bitch? You better let go of my best friend."

I used my forearm to hold my feisty best friend at bay. "Let's go," I told Mia.

"Just an FYI, Lucas has been fucking me *hard* for hours every night this week. He *really* knows what he's doing, but you already know that." The blond smiled, all sweet and full of poison. "If you think you're something special, you're not."

My heart fucking sank at her words. I yanked my arm from her grasp and continued toward the exit. She wasn't worth it. My lungs constricted even more, like a vise was crushing my chest. My blood pounded in my ears like a bass drum, and my breathing was shallow. As soon as we exited the building, I gasped for breath, taking in the polluted air of the city. It helped. It was better than being stuck in there, where the walls had started closing in on me from the moment I'd walked inside. *Fuck. Fuck.*

"Fuck!" I started walking. Didn't know where. Didn't care.

"Jules, wait." Mia's platforms clopped against the sidewalk as she fell into step with me. "Don't let that stupid bitch get to you. She's probably jealous."

"I don't care." It came out on my breath. "I don't care!" I screamed to the sky. "Lucas fucking Verduce can fuck whoever the fuck he wants. Including that blond bitch. I just . . . can't believe I was stupid enough to come here." Stopping, I hailed a cab. "The recital is in a week, and I really need to focus on that, so please don't encourage this anymore." I was fucking *done* with Lucas and his games.

She nodded and said nothing as a taxi pulled up. We both climbed in and headed back to my apartment, where a nice bottle of rosé awaited me.

Rehearsals for my spring recital filled the next week. I had to make sure my students were prepared to take the stage. They were all so excited for their first performance, and I couldn't deny that I was as well. A few of the parents commented on my performance in the music video. I even signed some autographs, which I thought was ridiculous.

Ethan and Lucas called and texted me nonstop, but I just ignored them. I didn't want to hear any-fucking-thing they had to say. My contract with them was over. They had no business trying to reach me anymore.

Mia suggested I hear them out, but I held my ground. *Fuck* them. I wanted to forget I'd ever met Lucas Verduce. Forget about that stupid contract. Forget that anything had ever happened between me and that rock star.

The evening of the recital arrived faster than I'd anticipated. I was a nervous wreck, mostly for my kids but somewhat for my solo, which I'd choreographed as the last number of the evening.

Mia scrambled around backstage with me, arranging the ten-year-olds for their performance. They looked so adorable in their pink leotards and tutus.

Mia walked up as the kids performed on the small wooden stage of the theater. "So . . . don't be mad."

I wanted to cuss at her but held my tongue. "What did you do now?" I crossed my arms.

With a wince, Mia met my stare. "I might've sort of told Kyle the details of your recital, which he then shared with Lucas, and they may or may not be in the audience right now."

Nostrils flared, I dropped my arms and stormed over to the curtain to peek out at the audience. Low and behold, Lucas, Kyle, and a few bodyguards were sitting in the front row. *Motherfucker.* My jaw clenched as I turned to face Mia.

"Are you mad?" she asked.

She knew damn well I was fucking livid. I didn't know how many times I'd stated that I did *not* want to see Lucas ever again. I moved to corral the twelve-year-old students in the dressing room.

"I'm sorry," she said, following me.

"Let's just get through this recital." My tone was sharp.

Her eyes widened, and she said nothing else as she helped me gather the students, leading them to the stage. I didn't know why he'd bothered to come. There was no fucking way I would give Lucas Verduce any more of my time.

CHAPTER 15

Lucas

S HE WAS PISSING ME THE FUCK OFF. I KNEW SHE WAS avoiding me. Hell, Mia hadn't even answered Ethan's calls or texts. Julia genuinely wanted nothing to do with me. It must've been the end of the world or some shit. I'd *never* had to work this hard for a woman's attention. Then again, I'd never wanted anyone like this before.

I hoped no one in the audience recognized me, though not because I didn't want to deal with fans. If news about me attending this ballet recital got out, it could ruin my reputation. Ethan definitely wouldn't be happy about that. I imagined what the tabloids would say.

ROCK STAR LUCAS VERDUCE ATTENDS BALLET RECITAL?

IS LUCAS V. TURNING IN HIS GUITAR FOR POINTE SHOES?

Mia walked out onto the stage and announced the last performance of the night. The lights dimmed. There were whispers among the audience. The music started, and it was Julia's audition song, "Diary of Jane" by Breaking Benjamin.

Julia's strong body twirled into the spotlight, her movements graceful and serene among the grit of the music. Her skin glistened with perspiration as she leaped across the stage. She made dancing appear effortless, but I knew firsthand it wasn't.

Her dark eyes were filled with passion and that fiery attitude. Watching her bare her soul made me want to feel that same passion about my music. I swallowed the lump in my throat as the song ended and she stood center stage, her chest heaving. In a city of thousands of people, Julia was the one I wanted.

After her performance, she walked onstage and thanked all the parents, friends, and family for their support. She said they should be proud of their kids and that she looked forward to the next recital. Throughout her entire speech, she didn't even bat an eye in my direction, but I swiped my lip ring, ready for the challenge.

Kyle leaned in and whispered, "I don't think you're gonna have much luck talking to her tonight."

I resisted the urge to flip him off, being surrounded by parents and all.

Once the theater had cleared out and the students were gone, Mia walked up to us in the front row. She hugged Kyle and greeted him with a kiss.

Poor girl. She probably thought she was getting him to commit. I didn't know how he felt about her, but I knew he hadn't stopped talking to his . . . groupies.

"She's in the dressing room. Whatever happens isn't my fault." Mia held her hands up in defense.

Got it. She meant that whatever reaction I got from Julia was all on me. After all, I had kind of crashed this thing. My heart pounded in my chest as I walked backstage, up a few steps, and into the surprisingly large dressing room. *Where is she?* I searched through the rows of white vanities lined up. She was in the last row, brushing out her long silky hair. Her chestnut eyes locked with mine. My heart sped up even more while a rush of blood flowed straight to my dick. *Fuck.* My body always knew what it wanted. What it craved.

"You're still here?" She shifted her gaze to the mirror and began wiping the heavy makeup from her gorgeous features. "What do you want?"

I took a few careful steps forward, knowing that she could snap at literally anything I had to say. I fucking lived for it. "I came to support you and your business. Even bought a ticket of my own." My fingers reached for the ticket stub in my right pocket, and I pulled it out and showed her in case she didn't believe me.

She didn't seem impressed. Suspicion was written all over her face. "Thanks."

"You did good out there." The urge to take her in my arms and kiss those delicious plump lips grew with each step I took toward her. She stood before me makeupless, in nothing but joggers, a loose tee, and black Chucks, and she'd never looked more fucking beautiful. My lips curved up.

Her brow furrowed. "Why don't you just tell me what

you want, Lucas?" She faced me after throwing the used wipes into the trash bin next to the vanity.

"Already told you."

She proceeded to grab her tote and a few other bags from the white laminate floor.

"Here, let me help—"

"I'm fine," she snapped, shouldering one duffel, then another.

Stubborn. So fucking stubborn.

My bodyguard fell into step as we made our way out of the dressing room. He stayed out of earshot, giving me and Julia privacy.

"Our music video is blowing up the charts, Sunshine," I said.

She stopped in her tracks. "You mean *your* music video?" It was more of a statement than a question.

"You were part of it too. It's as much yours as it is mine."

It was true, and the fans loved her in it. Interviewers had asked if she'd be going on tour with me or if she would be in any of my other music videos. I'd been evasive about the whole thing.

She just stood there staring at me, an unreadable look on her face.

"We're going on tour for three months. It wouldn't feel right if we went without you." Before she could respond, I added, "Ethan wrote a contract for you and everything. You'd be getting paid more." I was hoping that would sweeten the deal.

A look of uncertainty crept onto her face. "You can't

expect me to drop everything. No, I'm not doing it," she finally said.

I'd have been a lying fuck if I said that didn't sting a little. I studied her for a moment and knew from her fiery gaze there was nothing I could do to change her mind. Knowing that, I still fucking tried. "This money could help you pay for a bigger studio. You wouldn't be losing anything." At least, I didn't think she'd be.

"You can't just buy me out." If looks could kill, Julia's would've massacred me.

There was no mistaking that pissed-off look in her eyes. I just couldn't figure out why. Had I done something wrong?

"Why are you so pissed?" The corner of my mouth rose, and I leaned in. "Do you need me to fuck that little attitude out of you?"

She pursed her lips, eyes narrowing. "Please, Lucas, I don't need any more mediocre sex from you."

Without another thought, I grabbed her nape and pulled her close. Her hands braced against my chest. She thought it was mediocre? "Don't fuck with me, Sunshine. I'm not in the mood," I growled, inhaling her sweet, intoxicating scent.

Her brown eyes met mine. "No, Lucas. Don't fuck with *me*."

It came as no surprise she'd try to pick a fucking fight with me. Heat permeated my neck and chest. "Excuse me for thinking I was doing you a favor." Resisting the urge to press my lips to hers and push my tongue into her mouth, I released her, taking a few steps away.

"A favor?" She scoffed. "Nothing about what you're

offering screams 'favor,' and I don't need your fucking charity."

Where the hell was this all coming from? There had to be something else bubbling beneath the surface of her anger.

She tore her gaze away and let out a breath, crossing her arms. "You have my answer."

I knew she was shutting down and that I wouldn't get anything else out of her. "Well, you have my number if you change your mind."

An unfamiliar ache flared in my chest. When the fuck had I become the guy who got rejected by women? What twisted dimension was I living in? My bodyguard followed me out of the theater and opened the door of the parked SUV.

Kyle sat in the AC scrolling on his phone. I guessed Mia had gone back into the theater.

I settled into the back seat as Kyle asked, "How'd it go?"

Shaking my head, I replied, "Nope. She said she couldn't leave her business."

Thank fuck traffic had died down a bit. My bottle of Glenlivet sherry was awaiting me back at my penthouse. I was in desperate need of a glass or two . . . or three.

"Well, we don't leave until next weekend. Maybe she'll change her mind," Kyle said, gazing out his tinted window at the citizens walking the sidewalks of the commercial area we were passing through.

There was no way she would change her mind. Her ballet studio was just too important. My heart sank at the thought that maybe this was a sign to give up.

Lucas Verduce showing up at my fucking spring recital didn't surprise me. That little remark he made about fucking my attitude out of me didn't surprise me either. What took me by complete surprise was his offer to go on tour. I'd be getting paid more, but the idea of being on tour for three months, staying in hotels and cramped buses, sounded less than appealing. Anyway, I couldn't cancel all my classes and lessons, though what I'd be getting paid would more than cover for it.

Fuck me. And like he'd said, I could even afford to lease a bigger space with that money. *God, I'm so stupid.*

Wednesday came around. Classes and private lessons came and went. Neither Lucas nor Ethan had tried to contact me. Maybe Lucas had finally given up and realized I was a lost cause.

I should've been happy. I *was* happy. Yet something

didn't sit right with me. Was it the fact that I'd turned Lucas down without even considering his offer and how it could benefit me? Or was it the tinge of disappointment in his dark eyes? Maybe it was a bit of both.

"You're daydreaming again." Mia stood behind the reception desk, sorting through paperwork. She pushed her black reading glasses up the bridge of her nose. "You wanna talk about it?"

I continued wiping down the barre. "No, not really." Before she could say anything else, I asked, "Anyway, what's going on between you and Kyle?"

Her smile widened—if that was at all possible. "We're having fun right now. Haven't put a label on it or anything."

"Do you want to put a label on it?" I knew she could do one-night stands, but she wasn't the casual sex type. That was how it had started with her ex, Don.

She raised a shoulder. "I don't know. We're just feeling things out."

Oh no. I'd seen that look in her eyes before. "You're falling for him."

"I'm not," she whined.

"Goddammit, Mia." I really didn't want to see her get hurt by this guy, but she was going to do what she wanted. I let out a breath. "He's only going to break your heart. He's just like Lucas."

It was her turn to sigh. "Don't worry, Jules. I'm being careful."

I didn't say anything else about the matter. She was going to have to learn the hard way.

"I've been meaning to talk to you about something," she said.

That couldn't be good. "What is it?"

"I've been thinking about a career change. Don't get me wrong, this job is great, but I think I want to try something different," she said, still going through the papers on the desk.

My heart sank at her words, but I couldn't blame her for wanting to find something she was passionate about. "What were you thinking of doing?" If I were in her shoes and didn't like my job, I'd probably leave too.

"I don't know yet. I'm sure I'll know once I find it though. And don't worry, I'll find and train my replacement."

"I just want you to be happy, Mia, even if it's not with me." I immediately cringed at my own words.

She smiled. "God, you make it sound like we're breaking up."

The bells on the front door jingled.

"We're closed," I said without looking to the entrance.

"Hey, Jay Bird."

I peered up. "Pops? Is something wrong?" My heart skipped a beat as I left the rag on the barre. He almost never came to visit me at the studio. "Are you okay?" I walked up and examined him.

He grinned. "Yeah, I'm fine. I just wanted to take you to dinner if you're up to it."

Mia literally shooed me away, saying she'd lock up the studio.

For the first time in months, Dad and I had dinner. We

walked over to a popular Japanese hibachi place down the street. Dad loved sushi. I would order my usual: steak, rice, and veggies.

We sat in a booth in the somewhat-quiet restaurant and said nothing for the longest time. I took in the surroundings. The red brick walls were decorated with black-framed pictures of bamboo forests. There were hibachi grills on the other side of the restaurant. The soft light from the cast-iron fixtures above relaxed me. I'd been tense all day. *This is exactly what I need.*

After Dad sipped his water glass, he asked, "How're things going, Jay Bird?"

"Good, Pops. Really good," I replied after chewing and swallowing a chunk of red meat. God, I was such a fucking carnivore.

"Sorry I missed your recital. I'm sure it was fucking epic." He placed his hand on mine.

As much as I'd wanted him there, I understood why he hadn't made it: his band had a gig that night. "It's okay, Pops. I'm sure you guys had a great show, right?"

He nodded as he sat back in his seat. "Oh yeah, you know us. Rock out with our—"

I cleared my throat. "Family-friendly restaurant."

His mouth clamped shut, a grin creeping onto his features.

This place was great. I stuffed a few more bites of rice and meat into my mouth, observing the surroundings. They had a good dinner crowd going for them.

"So . . . Lucas Verduce." He clasped his hands on the tabletop.

And there went my mood. My lips pursed as I stopped eating. The sound of his name caused me to lose my appetite.

"What about him?" My voice was firm and full of warning.

Dad's brow rose. "Jay Bird, I don't think I've ever gotten that kind of a reaction from you just by saying a man's name."

"Yeah, well . . ." I blew out a sigh.

Before taking a bite of his food, Dad said, "He came and saw me after your recital last weekend."

I nearly spat my water out. "Wait, what? Lucas Verduce? Lead singer of No Blood, No Alibi?"

Dad shrugged like it was nothing. "It's starting to become a regular thing."

I dropped my wooden chopsticks onto my plate. Would I never be rid of that man? Maybe he was telling the truth when he'd said he liked my dad's band. I had no fucking idea. "And?"

"Said he liked my band and asked for advice on going independent."

Great. Soliciting information from my old man to get in his good graces.

"And . . ." Dad took another drink of water. He'd done that on purpose to leave me in suspense. *Guess that's why I'm drawn to assholes.* "He asked me to talk to you about some tour contract."

"I fucking knew it," I blurted a little too loud, and the other patrons looked my way. I mouthed, "I'm sorry," then turned my attention back to Dad.

"Family-friendly restaurant, Jules," he teased, that grin never leaving his face.

The waiter came and filled our glasses with ice water, then went on his way. I crossed my arms and inhaled. That fucking asshole had gone and told my dad like we were five years old or something. My heart thrummed in my chest as the urge to go to Lucas's penthouse and strangle him washed over me.

"Well?" I said.

"Well what?"

"Aren't you gonna give me the spiel about missing an opportunity of a lifetime?" I asked, uncrossing my arms.

He shook his head as he took another bite of his food. I gazed at my dad with a furrowed brow and waited for him to chew and swallow.

"I told him you're a grown woman and that you'd made your decision for a reason. I only hope you considered his offer before rejecting it." He gazed at me with his soft dark eyes.

Nope. I'd pretty much told him to fuck off without considering the options. My voice rose an octave. "Well . . ." I took a breath. "I mean, I do have my business to run."

He nodded like he wanted to say more but was biting his tongue on the matter.

"What?" I prodded.

"You think you'll regret turning him down?"

I already had. Dad sure knew how to get to me. Running my palms down my face, I didn't quite know how to respond to that, but I was pretty sure my silence spoke volumes.

"Jay Bird, I've always known you to play it safe, unlike me. The point is, don't let fear keep you from what you want in life. Or *who* you want." He held out his large hand.

My heart warmed as I placed mine in his and squeezed. Moments like this made me forget all the resentment I harbored for him.

Dammit. I blinked back tears at the sudden tug in my chest, looking away from the man who'd raised me.

Swallowing the lump in my throat, I asked, "What if I don't know what I want?"

"Look at me, Jay Bird."

I met Dad's eyes once more after letting out a long breath. Those eyes had seen so much, experienced so much. They were the same ones that had shed tears in front of me when Mom left. He always looked at me with so much pride, so much respect, so much fervor. I knew he loved me in spite of everything. I knew he would do anything for me.

Tears spilled from my eyes and down my cheeks, and I wiped them away with a napkin.

"I think you know what you want. You're just too damn stubborn and afraid to admit it." He reached across the table and swiped his thumb over my damp cheek.

Of course, Dad was right. He knew me like the back of his hand, but there was no way I would ever admit I had feelings for Lucas. No way would I put my heart on the line for someone who didn't even know the meaning of commitment. *No way.* If I was going to sign the contract, it would be for the money alone. Nothing else.

"And what do *you* think I want?"

He ran his fingers over the stubble on his jaw. "You want me to be honest, yeah?"

I held out my palm. "Please. You've been honest about everything else."

"You want *him*, Jay Bird. But you've guarded your heart so well, you won't let yourself feel that." He let out a breath and stared at his half-eaten plate of food. "Mom did a number on us. But . . . maybe it's time to open ourselves up again."

My eyebrows rose. I remained quiet. I'd had no idea that he had closed himself off too, though it made sense now why he let me have my independence at such a young age. It also made me wonder if that was the reason why he and Gale stayed friends.

With a faint smile, Dad changed the subject and talked about the old times, when his band was first starting out. The weather came up a few times, and after two hours, Dad paid the tab and walked me to my apartment.

Before he left me at my front door, he pulled me into an embrace. "Regardless of what choice you make, I *am* proud of you, my little Jay Bird. No bullshit."

"Thanks, Pops." I sank deeper into his hug, truly missing his warmth.

"Let me know what you decide." He let me go and started walking toward the staircase of my apartment building.

I rolled my eyes. "I think you already know."

He chuckled and said nothing as he made his way down to the lobby.

The next morning, I awoke to a phone call from Mia. I rubbed the sleep from my eyes and answered, "Hello?"

"We have an emergency at the studio." Her voice dripped with panic.

"I'm on my way." I threw on some joggers, a tee, and black sneakers before grabbing my tote and rushing out the door. *What the hell could the emergency be?* Mia had never sounded that frantic.

The taxi started to veer over on the side of the street in front of my studio building. I paid the driver and didn't even let him come to a complete stop before hopping out of the car. Rushing up to the building, I pulled the door open and stepped into icy ankle-deep water.

"What the fuck happened?" I screeched.

Mia rushed out from the back room with a dark-haired man, the landlord. Her jeans and baby-blue cardigan were soaked. "Oh my god, Jules. A pipe burst."

For once in my life, I had no words. All my hard work was drowning in this fucking water.

Glancing at the man standing beside Mia, I asked, "How long will it take to get the pipe fixed?" There were sounds of power tools and banging coming from the back room.

The landlord, Adam Riley, replied, "Well, there's some major corrosion, so I decided to take care of the issue before it causes a bigger problem. So, might be a while."

"Fuck." Maybe this was a sign from the universe, a big-ass "fuck you, Julia." I'd made my decision to accept Lucas's offer while talking with my dad the night before, but this solidified it even more. I just had to woman up and confront him about it. I knew Lucas's cocky ass wouldn't make it easy for me either.

Since Ethan was the band manager, I called him first. He told me to meet Lucas at his penthouse and that he'd send a car for me.

Here we fucking go. The ride to his huge penthouse building was definitely tense. I attempted Mia's breathing technique bullshit. Couldn't focus on shit. The fact of the matter was that my life was falling apart, and I was losing control. I watched buildings pass by through the tinted window of the car.

Twenty minutes passed, and the vehicle came to a stop in front of the familiar tall apartment building.

"We're here, Miss Blackwell," the driver said.

I gazed up at the sleek high-rise and climbed out of the car, thanking the driver. I rolled the tension from my shoulders and made my way into the modern lobby. I hadn't even bothered to change my clothes from this morning. My shoes were still wet from walking through my flooded studio. Oh well. He would just have to fucking deal with it.

The receptionist made a quick phone call, and before I knew it, I was in the metallic elevator heading up. The heater had to be on; my cheeks became hotter with each floor I passed. *Fuck, calm down. This is a business meeting.* The final ding of the elevator caused me to flinch, and then the doors rolled open. I half expected Lucas to be there, but he wasn't.

"Hello?" I walked through the closet, kicking off my shoes before heading down the long hallway. "Lucas?"

"I'm in here."

His familiar voice came from the kitchen at the end of the hallway on the right. Once I reached that point, the whole apartment opened up. It reminded me of the glass house in the movie *The Lake House*, but more modern and with lots of black. A typical bachelor pad. The kitchen was connected to the living and dining rooms. In the middle of it all was an electric fireplace.

"Hey, you hungry?"

Fuck me. My eyes roamed to Lucas, who stood in the kitchen in front of the stainless-steel stove, his hair all disheveled, a white hand towel draped across his tan shoulder. And yeah, no shirt. His upper body was laid bare for my eyes to drink up, and boy were they thirsty. Had he somehow gained more muscle since the last time I'd seen him? Then my gaze wandered down to those gray fucking sweatpants hanging low on his hips. To top it all off, he was barefoot. I bit my lip. Hard. *This is business.*

He turned, and those russet eyes met mine. "Well?"

Yup, as I expected, that signature roguish grin formed on his handsome features.

Lucas knew exactly what he was doing. My eyes narrowed as I pulled out a stool and sat at the kitchen island. I glanced at the clock on my phone. It was after five. Hadn't even grasped that much time had passed already.

"I could eat." The savory smell of beef filled my nostrils. *I thought he didn't eat red meat?*

"It's stir-fry. I know you like your steak." He winked at me, and I just about turned to liquid.

Dammit, had I told him about that?

"Smells good." God, what was happening here? Were we getting along for once?

He faced me after plating the food and placing a serving in front of me.

I stared down at my hands. "Listen, I'm sorry about going off on you at the theater."

"Don't worry about it. I'm used to being yelled at. Ethan does it all the time," he mused with the wave of his hand.

I picked up a whiff of his vanilla-and-cedar scent. Why'd he have to smell so fucking good? Without thinking, I asked, "Could I have a glass of water?" Just so he'd get away from me and I wouldn't be tempted to jump his sexy bones.

"So, Ethan told me you reconsidered our offer." He passed me a bottled water, then sat on the stool next to me.

God, the food was either actually good or I was fucking hungry. The meat melted in my mouth, and the vegetables had the right amount of crisp to them. The flavors were well-balanced and weren't overpowering. I glared daggers at him.

He noticed and cocked an eyebrow. "What?"

"This is good."

"Why are you so surprised?" There was a tinge of amusement in his voice.

Why *was* I so surprised? Probably because none of the guys I'd dated could cook for shit. Granted, I wasn't the best cook either, but I'd done all the cooking in most of my short-term relationships. Thankfully, it wasn't my cooking that had scared them off. They wanted to settle down, and I didn't have the time for that.

"Just didn't expect this from you," I replied before taking another spoonful into my mouth. A moan escaped me. *Fuck.*

He smiled in silence. No dirty comment. Nothing. "Let's go over this contract real quick."

I nodded, my mouth full. "Okay."

"I'll be right back." He padded down the hall, leaving me alone to finish the rest of my dinner.

When he came back, I asked, "Did you eat already?"

"Yeah, I had my meal prep before you arrived." He grinned, holding up a manila folder.

Wait a damn minute. "Did you cook this just for me?" I tilted my head.

He had a clueless look on his handsome face, like he didn't see an issue with cooking me dinner. I wondered if he did this for all his girls, especially that blond leggy woman who'd confronted me at the concert. *That bitch.*

"I figured you'd been working all day and didn't have time to eat." He opened the envelope and placed the contents in front of me. It was only a few pages. He took out a black pen, and our fingers brushed as he handed it to me.

I ignored the tingle his touch had caused. "You'd be wrong about that."

"About what? You working all day?" He sat next to me.

"Yeah . . ." I drew out the word, debating whether I should tell him about my studio. "My landlord discovered an issue in my building. Long story short, my studio will be closed for a while."

What was that look on his face? Disappointment? I decided not to prod.

"What about your students?"

"Mia and I called them and explained the issue." Thankfully, the parents of my kids loved my teaching methods and said they'd continue doing business with me despite the circumstances.

"That must've been a task," he remarked.

Honestly, that had probably been the most tiring part of the day, having to explain the same thing over and over again. I cleared my throat and read through the contract.

It would be three months, and I wouldn't get paid if I didn't perform at all shows. I'd only dance when the band played "My Crimson Love." Choreography would be provided. All travel arrangements would be paid for by the label, etcetera. When I didn't see any issues, I signed the document in the designated areas, then slid the papers over to him.

"Is that all you need from me?" I stood from the barstool, putting distance between us.

"For now." He ran his tongue over his lip ring, and I instantly remembered the cool metal against my mouth. It had sent a cool shiver down my spine as he'd fucked me. I had to get out of there.

I started backing away. "Well, if that's all, I'll be on my way." When I reached the walk-through closet and realized he hadn't followed, my nerves settled. After I slipped my shoes on, I walked out to the elevator. But before I could press the button, a strong hand grabbed my forearm and spun me around. My back hit the metal sliding doors as I came face-to-face with Lucas.

"The fuck you are."

His mouth fell onto mine, and my mind went blank. He pushed his hard body against me, pinning me against the cold surface. His hands roamed down my sides all the way to the backs of my thighs. He spread my legs and lifted me with ease onto his hips, never breaking the kiss. I moaned into his mouth as he pressed his arousal against my warm center.

"Fuck, Julia. I want you," he whispered against my neck.

The memory of what that leggy blond had said flooded my mind. *Lucas has been fucking me hard for hours every night this week.* I pushed him away and stared at him. His gaze was filled with desire and something else I couldn't quite put my finger on.

"What does that mean?" I asked, unwrapping my legs from around his waist, landing on my sneaker-clad feet.

His brow wrinkled as he contemplated my question. "I thought I was clear."

"No. You have *never* been clear about this." I gestured a finger between us.

He rubbed the back of his neck. "I don't know, Sunshine," he muttered.

"What don't you know? Why can't you be honest with me?" I said, crossing my arms.

His eyes narrowed. "Me be honest?" He scoffed. "You're the one not being honest."

"You want me to be honest? Fine. If we're going to be stuck touring together, this can't happen again." I had to set boundaries with him. I *had* to keep him at a distance, regardless of my attraction to him, regardless of my . . . feelings.

He didn't say anything for the longest time. Had he shut down? Then, after another minute of deafening silence, he said, "I'm sorry."

I let out a breath and hit the button for the elevator.

"Just . . . don't go. Stay. We can watch a movie or something, and I promise I'll keep my hands to myself." He raised his hands, then stuffed them into his pockets.

He wanted me to stay and watch a movie? This had to be some kind of trick or something. When we'd filmed the music video together, I'd always thought he hung around me because we worked together. Did he honestly want my company, or was he simply lonely?

"A movie?" I asked, crossing my arms over my chest. Was he even capable of having a platonic relationship with the opposite sex?

"Yeah." He grinned, and I really wished he wouldn't because my stupid heart fluttered every damn time.

The elevator door dinged open. I stood there like an idiot, contemplating whether I should take him up on his offer. *A movie wouldn't hurt.* The door slid shut, and there went my opportunity for an escape.

I pointed my index finger in his face. "Fine, but if you try anything, I'm kneeing you in the balls."

He swatted my hand away and chuckled, shaking his head. "Whatever you say, Sunshine."

For the first time in a long time, I was *just* hanging out with a girl. No, not a girl. A woman. And not just any woman. Julia Blackwell, the epitome of frustration, both mentally and physically, and the reason I'd been sleeping and eating like shit. *Fuck.* I had it bad for her. I was so pathetically infatuated. And the worst part was that I was willing to have her in my life without *having* her. At least that was what I kept telling myself.

"I can't believe you picked *this* movie," Julia said as she sat comfortably on the couch inches from me.

Honestly, I hadn't even been paying attention to the classic movie playing on my flat screen. "Tell me you've seen it."

She glanced at me with narrowed eyes. "Yes, I've seen *Jurassic Park*. It's one of my favorites."

I wanted to know all her favorites. The corner of my mouth rose.

Just because I'd agreed to be friends didn't mean I had to stop wanting her. And I knew she wanted me. I could tell in the way she'd kissed me, in the way she'd wrapped her legs around my waist while we made out in front of the elevator. Something was holding her back, and I was going to figure it out.

"So, how'd you get into teaching ballet?" I lowered the volume of the TV.

She hugged one of my blue throw pillows to her chest. "Well . . . I used to go to the nearby community center to dance. It was kind of like therapy for me and a way to figure out what I wanted to do next. I knew my body wouldn't be the same after my injury. One of the staff asked if I'd be interested in teaching their dance class. I needed a job, so I agreed, and the rest was history."

I couldn't help shifting toward her. This woman was like a magnet. "So, it was basically an accident?"

She let out a short laugh. "Yeah, I guess." Her eyes met mine, and I noticed the circle of light brown around her irises. "What about you?"

"What about me?" I glanced at the TV. The dinosaurs were loose and running rampant on the island.

"How'd you get into rock stardom?" Her body turned toward me as the movie continued to play in the background.

I shrugged, not sure how to answer that question. "It just kinda happened."

She raised an eyebrow. "Okay. Did you always want to be a rock star?"

"Not really. Just loved music and writing lyrics, I guess."

"What do you love about it?" she asked.

God, what was with all the tough questions? I hadn't really thought about it.

The T. rex roared as I mulled over my answer.

"I guess . . ." Too embarrassed to face her, I rested my head on the cushion of the couch, looking toward the high ceiling of the penthouse. "I love that music tells a story. It's a way to bare your soul to people, letting them know how you truly feel without actually telling them." I wasn't sure if that made sense. "Kinda like dance. Except, you tell a story with your body."

She didn't say anything for the longest time, and I didn't know what to make of her silence. Did she think I was bullshitting her?

"Did you fall asleep over there?" I glanced at her. She was staring at me.

"I should go."

"Did I say something wrong?" My brows ruffled as I stood and followed her to the elevator.

"No. I realized I have a lot to do before we hit the road." She pressed the button.

Something I'd said must've scared her. I wondered if how I felt about music was how she felt about dancing. If that was the case, why did she feel the need to run away?

"Okay. I'll have a car pick you up at your apartment on Friday."

She nodded as the elevator door opened. "Sounds good."

She stepped in, and I wanted to pull her back out. I

didn't want her to go, but I had to respect that she needed her space.

"Have a good night, Sunshine." Her gentle smile imprinted in my mind before the door slid closed. And I was left alone in my huge penthouse, thoughts of her haunting me.

A few hours before our first show of the Crimson Love tour, I paced around backstage, waiting for Ethan. He was supposed to be making certain arrangements for me. Well, for Julia. She didn't know it yet, and I couldn't wait to see the look on her face.

Ethan finally walked through the back entrance in his black blazer and jeans. "I took care of the tickets. Mia is taking care of the rest."

"Are you sure?" I asked. It was unlike him to push his tasks onto someone else.

He nodded. "Positive. It's in the bag."

Mia seemed like the responsible, reliable type, so I let it go.

Seats in the huge amphitheater filled up, except for one section to the right of the stage where I knew Julia would be dancing. It was thirty minutes to showtime, and she was warming up in a little corner by herself, headphones on her ears. She was getting in the zone, and I respected that, keeping my distance.

I did a few jumping jacks and push-ups to get my blood flowing and the nerves under control. The MC walked onstage to hype the audience up and announce the band. I looked out at the crowd once more, and my eyes locked onto the section to the right of the stage. Mia and a group of young children mixed with adults walked down the side aisle and took their seats. A schoolboy smile crept onto my face at the moment I caught a glimpse of Julia's students' shining faces. I was glad we'd decided to contract Mia as an assistant manager for the tour.

Thirty minutes into our last set, sweat coated my body as I strummed my electric guitar. It was the second-to-last song, and my heart was pumping, adrenaline coursing through my veins. Lost in the music, the audience screamed and cheered and bounced to the rhythm of the beat.

Finally, we played "My Crimson Love," and I introduced Julia on the stage. Her hands were clasped in front of her, and there was nervousness in those gorgeous eyes of hers. I smiled at her and gestured toward the section where her students sat. She looked, and they waved and screamed along with the rest of the audience.

Julia's smile reached her eyes as the music began. She glanced at me with a gracious grin, then started to dance. I would've given up all my talent if that meant I was the reason behind her smiles. The question was, would she let me?

After the show, Mia took the kids and their parents backstage to meet the band. I was surprised by how well my fellow band members interacted with them, especially Kyle. He was really good with the kids, giving them piggyback rides and talking to them about his favorite guitar.

I stood back to observe the scene and smiled. Julia was glowing, and I was falling even more for her.

Her eyes met mine as she strode toward me and wrapped her arms around my neck, pulling me against the curves of her body. I returned her embrace, losing myself in her warmth.

"Thank you," she whispered into my ear, her breath tickling my skin.

I squeezed her a little tighter. "You're welcome." This woman had me wrapped around her finger, and she didn't even know it. "Why don't you show them our buses? I'm sure they'd love that." I needed to get away from her before I did something I'd regret.

"Really?" She released me, her mouth curved up.

"Yeah, I'll let security know."

"Okay." She rushed back to the group and asked them if they wanted to see the buses. They went crazy and were so excited, like they'd never been on luxury tour vehicles before. I crossed my tatted arms over my chest and grinned as they walked away. From that moment on, I knew I was done for.

It had been a while since I'd felt satisfied with any performance, but having Julia on tour with us gave us the edge we needed, the edge *I* needed.

There were two luxury buses and one box truck for our instruments and equipment. Lita, Mia, and Julia stayed in one, and I was stuck with a bus full of dudes: Ethan, Kyle, Mark, and Billy. I spent most of my time in the back room writing and playing my acoustic guitar. I didn't know why, but I'd been on a roll with the song writing. Okay, maybe I knew why . . .

Ethan walked in. It smelled like the guys had been drinking and smoking in the lounge area. "Hey, would you stop being fucking broody and take a shot with us?" He leaned against the small doorframe.

The truth was, I hadn't felt like doing the usual boozing and smoking on this tour. I'd gone on many tours throughout my music career, but this was the first time I'd been somewhat sober. "Not tonight, man."

He frowned. "We're a month into the tour, and you haven't had a single drop of alcohol."

"Not true," I said. "Had a drink the other night when we made an appearance at that lounge." It had been a virgin drink, but still counted.

He crossed his arms. "I'm not leaving until you take *one* shot with us."

I'd known this would happen eventually, so I indulged

him and joined the guys up front. I threw back one shot with them, then another. Soon I was about ten shots in and felt pretty fucking good—so good that I decided to text Julia. Her bus was following ours, it was about midnight, and we were thirty minutes from our hotel in Baltimore. We'd packed up and left late from our last gig in Philadelphia.

ME

You danced well tonight.

What was I thinking when I texted her that? Of course she'd danced well. She was a professional, had trained at Julliard for Christ's sake. *Idiot.*

A few minutes passed before she responded.

JULIA

Thanks. I enjoyed your guys' performance too.

ME

So . . . what're you girls doing back there?

JULIA

We're in some sexy lingerie having a pillow fight.

Dammit. She was fucking with me. I couldn't help but grin as I responded.

ME

You do know Lita swings both ways, right?

JULIA

How do you know I don't?

My eyes narrowed on my screen as I sat on the cushy seats of the lounge in the bus.

ME

Do you?

If she did, that meant I'd have to work twice as hard. My phone buzzed while I contemplated that.

JULIA

No, I don't. Anyway, why are you texting me?

ME

I can't text a friend?

JULIA

Didn't know we were. This is the first time you've texted me since we left NYC.

ME

Yeah . . . sorry. Kinda been in my own head lately.

It wasn't a lie. All I did was perform, do interviews, make appearances at parties, and then go to sleep in the back of the bus or hotel room.

She didn't respond, so I texted her again.

ME

You still there?

JULIA

Yeah. Sorry. Lita just gave me this fruity
shot concoction.

ME

You're drinking?

I'd kind of figured she'd stay away from alcohol for a while after that last incident.

JULIA

Yeah, isn't that what you're supposed to
do on tours?

ME

Not necessarily.

Since she'd been drinking, I decided to take advantage of the situation.

ME

So . . . why ballet?

I looked up to see Ethan passed out next to me and Billy lying on the carpeted floor with his forearm covering his face. Mark was sitting on the other couch, watching TV. I hadn't seen where Kyle had gone, but if I had to guess, he'd probably gone to his bunk.

JULIA

It's simple really. Ballet was there for me
when my mom left. I was only twelve.
Ballet was there for me when my dad got
busy with his band. Honestly, it's the only
thing that hasn't failed me.

God, I wanted to hug her. But not because I pitied her. It was more out of admiration. She'd learned how to make a shitty situation better for herself. When my mom died, I'd turned to music, but I'd also acted out. I'd started acting like the typical rock star way before the fame and money.

ME

I kinda wish I could hug you right now.

Why I'd texted her *that* was beyond me. Probably the alcohol talking.

JULIA

Why?

ME

Why not?

JULIA

Kind of random, don't you think?

ME

Not really. After what you just texted me.

JULIA

Well. Maybe I'll give you one. If you're lucky.

For some fucking reason, that last text had me giddy like a schoolgirl. It was just a hug. It wasn't like I was going to get laid or anything. What the hell was this chick doing to me?

We arrived at our hotel, and Ethan checked us in, still buzzed. He gave the girls a card key, then the crew. As usual, I'd be sharing a room with Ethan, Billy, Mark, and Kyle. I really wanted to see Julia though. Even though it was close to two in the morning, I was wide-awake, and I didn't think we had anything scheduled the next day.

With liquid courage still coursing through my veins, I shot Julia a text.

ME

Hey, you haven't gone to bed yet, have you?

A few seconds later, she texted back.

JULIA

No. Why?

ME

Meet me in the lobby.

JULIA

It's late.

ME

So? You got a hot date in the morning?

JULIA

What if I do?

I had no right to be upset if she did, but still. A tinge of jealousy crept through me, making my blood boil.

JULIA

Give me ten minutes.

My heart leaped out of my chest after I read her response. "I'm going down to the lobby."

Billy and Mark were already knocked out, sharing one of

the two queen-size beds. Ethan had gone into the huge suite bathroom for a shower. Kyle lay on a rollaway bed next to the window. He was the only one awake on his phone, probably texting Mia or some other groupie chick.

"Cool. Don't do anything I wouldn't do," he said.

"That isn't saying much." I headed to the door and walked out in some dark sweats and a hoodie.

The hotel we were staying at was historic and used to be an old pier on the Patapsco River in Baltimore. It was probably the most luxurious hotel I'd stayed in. My heart thrummed in my chest as I walked down the grand staircase to the lobby.

Where is she? My eyes scanned the space until they finally landed on her. Julia sat on one of the plush modern chairs in black joggers and a gray long-sleeve shirt. Her hair was swept up in a messy bun, and damn . . . She was fucking beautiful.

I sat in the seat next to her. "Fancy meeting you here."

She looked up at me from her phone and smiled. "Hey."

"So, how're you liking the tour so far?" I leaned back in the seat with my arms crossed. They had the AC blasting, and it sent chills rippling down my spine.

"It's fine, I guess. Didn't think I'd be so tired." She stuffed her phone into her pocket. "The girls are kind of driving me crazy."

My buzz was starting to wear off. "Well, if you ever want to stay in my bus, you're welcome to. I'll send one of the guys over."

Her eyebrows rose. Maybe that had come out wrong.

"Promise to keep my hands to myself." I raised my hands.

Her lips curved into that heart-melting smile I loved. "I might take you up on your offer."

"Yeah?"

"Yeah, why not? We're friends now, right?" she said, and I stopped myself from wincing.

"Yeah. Friends." What was I doing? I didn't want *just* a friendship with her. I feigned a grin.

Silence ensued between us before Julia asked, "So, why the guitar?"

I looked down at the dark carpeted floors of the lobby. She was just getting me back for questioning her about ballet earlier.

"Well . . . my mom was into music. Loved all types and was always singing. She taught me how to play. When I was eleven, she was diagnosed with cancer. It was too late for her to receive treatments, so I . . ." God, this was hard to talk about. I swallowed a lump in my throat before I continued. "I basically had to watch her die. I guess I chose the guitar because it keeps me close to her and helps me cope with her absence."

I didn't want to look Julia in the eyes. What if she thought I was pathetic? Fuck, my eyes were watery. *Damn allergies.*

Arms wrapped around my shoulders, and my head fell against Julia's chest. She was hugging me from the side of the seat. It was a bit awkward, but I worked with it.

"Uh . . . Julia?" I said as she embraced my head closer to

her bosom, her heartbeat pounding in my ear.

"Shh, don't ruin this." She stroked the side of my head like I was some kind of pet.

"This is weird," I blurted out with a grin, which caused her to push me away. I peered up at her standing next to me. Her eyes expressed irritation.

"Excuse me for trying to be nice." She placed a hand on her hip.

My lips curved up as I stood and placed the back of my hand on her forehead. "You feeling all right?"

Her eyes narrowed as she pulled away. "Fuck you."

"There she is." I chuckled.

She plopped back into the chair, and I sat down again.

"So, what do you like about teaching ballet?" I asked.

With a finger to her chin, she sat there thinking. "I guess I would like dance to mean something to them. A way to express themselves and deal with things that may be happening in their lives."

My brows rose. I hadn't expected that response, but it made sense, and it just made me want her more. God, this woman was amazing.

"What?" She shifted in her seat.

"Nothing." Realizing I'd been staring, I looked away. How the fuck was I supposed to stay friends with this woman? This was what she wanted, and I needed to respect that. But the thought of her with someone else set my insides on fire.

For the rest of the night, we just talked. She told me what it was like being raised by her dad, Rick. I spouted about what it was like raising myself after Mom died and having everything and nothing at the same time.

Before I knew it, the sun had begun its ascent over the horizon. The orangey-gold beams shone through the many paned windows of the lobby. I stared at Julia as she admired the ambiance. In the sunlight, her irises had a ring of gold around them. Her honey-beige skin seemed to glow despite the tiredness on her face. And those fucking plump dusty-rose lips.

Friends. Right. We'll see how long this lasts.

WHEN WE ARRIVED IN GREENSBORO, LUCAS AND I HAD an interview with the press addressing our relationship status. There'd been a few rumors going around about us secretly dating. Lucas stated we were just friends enjoying each other's company. I essentially told them the same thing in my own way.

Despite my and Lucas's blossoming friendship, he still found ways to aggravate me. After the band's first rehearsal, he started a water balloon fight backstage. At the end of it all, most of us were drenched. Okay, maybe it had been more fun than aggravating, but I still felt the need to act like I was annoyed with him. Pretending became more difficult with each second I spent in his presence.

After I changed and showered in the hotel room, my phone buzzed with a text from Lucas. He told me we had to make an appearance at some house party. I'd been looking forward to staying in. We'd been attending interviews and parties nonstop, and it was starting to get fucking old.

"Did Lucas tell you about the party tonight?" Lita walked in from the bathroom, and Mia lay next to me on one of the two queen-size beds.

I gave her a sheepish nod, elevating my leg on two of the hotel pillows. Since I'd been dancing so much, my old injury was flaring up more regularly. It wouldn't keep me from taking the stage, as long as I iced it after each show.

"What's wrong? You don't want to go?" Lita asked as she rummaged through her duffel bag, looking for an outfit.

Mia stared at her phone screen and said, "Looks like I'll have to meet you two there. Ethan needs me to do a few things beforehand."

"He's been making you do a lot of running around lately." Lita studied my best friend. "Want me to kick his ass?"

Mia laughed and shook her head.

I couldn't help but let out a chuckle as well.

"No, I like it. Keeps me busy." Mia stood and fixed herself in the mirror by the door before walking out of the room.

"He's working her like a dog," Lita remarked.

Mia had basically signed up to be an errand girl, but she seemed to enjoy it—especially the fact that she had easy access to Kyle. I could tell she was getting lost in the fairy tale of a committed relationship with him, but I'd already warned her about his type. *I hope she knows what she's doing.*

"We should probably head out. I think it's about an hour drive from here," Lita said, throwing on a crop top tee, baggy jeans, and sneakers.

I wore a plaid button-down over my black tank, skinny jeans, and Chucks. The guys had tried to "advise" me on my style choices, but I wasn't going to change for anyone. Besides, the fans seemed to like my grungy look.

Lita and I left for the party an hour after the boys had. I liked to say we were fashionably late. It wasn't like I wanted to be at that fucking party anyway. There were plenty of things I *didn't* want to do on this tour, but the record company was paying for my time, so I couldn't complain.

The driver pulled up to a beautiful white colonial-style house with huge round pillars and long rectangular windows. I didn't know who lived here. If I had to guess, they probably knew the producer or one of the executives at the label, but I wasn't sure.

Loud music thumped from the large house as Lita and I made our way up the steps of the porch. Lucas and the others were probably already halfway drunk.

I entered the house, and strobe lights lit the way through the foyer. People danced and ground against each other in whatever space was available. The music bumped so loud I could feel it pulsing through me.

When I glanced into the living room, my eyes locked onto Lucas and the guys, dancing and drinking their bottled beers.

Lita elbowed me and shouted, "They look like a bunch of kangaroos."

I laughed but stopped immediately when that fucking blond chick from that first concert walked up and draped herself over Lucas's shoulder, whispering something in his ear.

I need fucking alcohol. As if the universe had heard my thought, a handsome man with a platter of clear shooters walked up to me and Lita and offered us some. I double fisted that shit, pouring both down my throat.

"Go Jules! Come on, there's a dance floor outside." Lita led me out to the patio in the backyard, where more partygoers danced. On the way out, I took two more tequila shooters.

My mind and body were soon lost in the rhythm of the music. My hands trailed up my sides, and I stretched them above my head. I was floating on clouds, light as a feather, drifting through the writhing bodies, perspiration dripping down my temples.

Where the hell did Lita go?

A hand gripped my waist, and I was pulled against a hard chest. Another shot appeared in front of my face.

"Dance with me," a familiar voice whispered in my ear.

I drank the shot, then turned, vision askew. It was Lucas.

How the fuck did he find me? At some point during the night, I had shed my plaid shirt, which left me in just the black tank and skinny jeans. My hair hung in waves, cascading down my shoulders. *Damn, should've brought a hair tie.*

I kept my back to him and decided to punish him a little. Mischief curved my lips as I ground against him to the beat of the music. My heart skipped when his strong arms wrapped around my waist. I bit my bottom lip, relishing the hard length of him against me. Slipping through his arms, I sank into a deep squat, then slid my ass up his lean body.

His hand reached around, gripping the front of my neck, pulling me flush against his chest. His lips brushed the shell of my ear as he said, "We're going to have fucking problems if you keep doing that."

"Sounds like a personal problem," I said.

He released me, and I wasted no time in walking off the dance floor into the noisy house.

Why did he have to come along and ruin my vibe? The thought of him and that fucking blond chick plagued me as I made my way up the staircase of the house. Her words echoed in my head: *Lucas has been fucking me hard for hours every night this week.*

Shit, I didn't want to think about that. A lump formed in my throat as I burst through one of the doors on the second floor. Thankfully, no one was in there having sex. I was sober enough to notice the modern rustic design of the space. The bed had a black iron frame. A dresser stood against the wall below the small rectangular window, and there was a desk with a chair in one corner. It could've been a guest room with the minimal decor.

After shutting the door, I plopped onto the enormous bed, desperate for the room to stop spinning. My warm body sank into the plush mattress and pillows and before I knew it, the alcohol lulled me to sleep.

THERE HAD TO HAVE BEEN A FUCKING HAMMER BANGING on my head. That was the only explanation for the throbbing. Granted, it wasn't as bad as last time. My tolerance was going up. Still, I really shouldn't have drunk that much. The sun shining through the window of the room didn't help.

The bed dipped and rattled, and the movement caused me to jump. I looked to see what or who was causing it. *For fuck's sake.* It was Lucas. Sound asleep next to me without a care in the world. I hoped to God no one knew about this.

There was a knock at the door, and the muffled voice of Ethan rang through. "Julia? Lucas?"

"Yeah?" I answered, sitting up and swinging my legs over the edge of the mattress, my bare feet hitting the cold hardwood floor.

"Is Lucas in there with you?" Ethan asked.

Dread consumed my body. I had no idea how Lucas was sleeping through all this.

Biting the inside of my cheek, I replied, "Yeah, he is."

"Thank God." Ethan let out a sigh. "There's a car coming for us. Should be here in about ten minutes."

"Okay, we'll be ready." I picked up one of the plush pillows and flung it at Lucas.

He grunted, and his eyes peeled open, squinting from the beams of sunlight streaming through the window. "What the fuck?"

I straightened, slipping on my socks and green sneakers. "Get up. Ethan has a car coming to pick us up." He was lucky I didn't throw my shoe at his pretty face. Honestly, he probably would've liked that. *Fucker.* Without another word, I walked out of the room.

Mia waited for me at the top of the staircase, a smug smile on her face. Her hair was styled in a messy bun, which only meant one thing: she'd been thoroughly fucked. "Someone had a good time last night."

"You wouldn't happen to have Tylenol, would you?" I rubbed my temples in a circular motion with my middle and index fingers. "Also, where the fuck were you last night?"

Mia uncrossed her arms and fell into step with me, and we made our way downstairs. "First of all, good morning to you too. There's Tylenol at the hotel. Second of all, I was with Kyle."

I huffed. "Of course."

"You're one to talk," she retorted, following me through the foyer. Maids were cleaning up the aftermath of the party. There were shot glasses, red cups, streamers, and used napkins everywhere.

"Nothing happened between me and Lucas last night. In fact, I went to sleep alone," I said, opening the front door of the house.

Mia looked at me like she didn't believe me. "You don't have to lie."

"I'm not." I pinched the bridge of my nose. "Can we not do this right now?"

"Fine, but this isn't over," she said.

The rest of the band members were already on the sidewalk, waiting. Ethan must've had multiple cars coming. I stood back, away from the group. They all had knowing looks on their faces, and I couldn't help but roll my eyes. I was pretty sure everyone waiting had gotten laid, except for me and Lucas, and probably Ethan too. As we continued waiting in hungover silence, Lucas finally walked out of the house.

"Did you two have fun last night?" Billy asked, a coy smile on his rugged face.

"Shut the fuck up," Lucas rasped.

Billy held his hands up in surrender and backed away.

Lucas and I rode in different cars on the way back to the hotel; he must've sensed that I needed some space. It wasn't enough that I had to see him at rehearsals, shows, interviews, *and* everything in between. The truth was, we were all probably getting on one another's nerves, but that was to be expected. We spent nearly every waking hour together.

I walked into the hotel room and threw myself onto the bed in the fetal position. Mia was buying me some Tylenol and bottled water from the small store in the lobby. Lita headed for the shower, so it was just me. Alone. In the mind-numbing silence.

I stared at my phone sitting on the square bedside table. It vibrated, alerting me to an incoming text message. I turned away from it, ignoring the buzz. Then it pulsed again. With an aggravated groan, I reached over and grabbed it.

LUCAS

Are you mad at me? Did I do something wrong?

Was he fucking kidding? My eyes narrowed as I worked my fingers across the keyboard.

ME

I'm fine.

LUCAS

The guys think we fucked. Maybe we should've.

I rolled my eyes.

ME

How about no.

LUCAS

Damn, was I that bad? Haven't you ever heard of friends with benefits?

My jaw clenched.

ME

Why don't you get what you want from that blond whore you were with last night?

I almost hit send but realized it made me sound like a jealous fucking girlfriend. Instead, I erased that last message and typed another.

ME

Like I said before, NO.

LUCAS

Lol. I'm teasing you, Sunshine. It looks like we have a little bit of time on our hands in the next city. You wanna hang out?

My brow rose.

By hang out, you mean sit in the lobby and talk?

LUCAS

Nah, I rented a car for us to explore the city. So, how 'bout it?

Mia walked through the door with Tylenol, water, and a cupcake, and I practically mauled her for it. I immediately swallowed two pills and guzzled down half of the huge bottle. For me, the cream-filled minicake was a remedy for hangovers.

"Someone's thirsty," she mused. "So, you ready to admit you had sex with Lucas yet?"

"For fuck's sake, Mia. Let it go." I let out a breath and looked at my phone, Lucas's question still on the screen. I decided I needed a change of scenery and time away from Mia's prodding. So, without further hesitation, I responded to Lucas.

ME

Yeah, sounds good.

He sent back a smiley face, and I couldn't help but think I might regret this decision.

THE SPORTS CAR I'D RENTED WAS WAITING AT THE HOTEL when we arrived. Once the buses were parked, Ethan tossed me a set of keys, and I texted Julia to meet me in the back of the building where the car was parked. I watched the sun setting on the horizon while waiting for her.

I still didn't know why Julia was angry, and it annoyed the fuck out of me. It wasn't like I'd fucking taken advantage of her. I'd literally *just* slept next to her. Granted, I could've chosen one of the other eight bedrooms in that house, but drunk me had wanted to be near her. Hell, sober me wanted to be near her.

What the fuck am I going to do once the tour ends? I had to tell her the truth. But I didn't know if I could handle the rejection now that I'd gotten to know her better. It seemed she liked to keep me at arm's length. We were more than halfway through the tour, and I was running out of time.

Julia walked out the back door of the tall building, her gaze searching the parking lot. She looked so fucking cute. Her hair was in that notorious messy bun, and she wore her usual grunge attire with one of those black Velcro knee braces around her right leg. She hid pain well, but all I wanted to do was take it away completely. As she walked closer, I noticed black liner around her beautiful brown eyes.

I opened the passenger door of the coupe, and her gaze narrowed on me like I'd done something wrong.

"Where are we going?" She stopped a few feet away, folding her arms over her chest.

"It's a surprise." I smirked. "What? You don't trust me?"

She stepped forward without a word and sat in the seat. I made sure her leg was out of the way before closing the door and making my way to the driver's side.

It had been a while since I'd driven a car like this, and I was going to cherish every moment. I sped through the city, taking full advantage of the horsepower at my fingertips. Julia sat next to me in silence, admiring the sights. I had AC/DC playing on the radio and caught her tapping her fingers on her leg to the beat.

I turned the volume down. "So . . . now that we know each other better, did you always want to be a dancer?" I asked, glancing at her.

She pursed her lips. "No." Her mouth curved up. "I actually wanted to be a zoologist."

That wasn't the answer I'd been expecting. I let out a soft chuckle. "Really? Like you wanted to work with animals?"

"Yeah. Don't judge me. What did *you* want to be?" She angled her body toward me and stared.

I answered without hesitation. "An astronaut."

She burst out in a giggling fit, making my heart beat faster. God, I loved her laugh.

"Glad I can amuse you."

Once she'd calmed down, she asked, "Why didn't you?"

"Why didn't I become an astronaut?" I cocked a brow, keeping my eyes on the darkened road ahead.

"Yeah."

I didn't know what to think. She actually thought I could do that? Her simple question sent warmth through my heart.

"Well . . . I fell in love with music." I shrugged and shot her a sidelong glance. "You can actually see me as an astronaut?"

She studied me. "Who am I to put limits on your aspirations? My dad always told me that if I wanted something bad enough, I could have it. It would just take a lot of work."

"Your dad's a smart guy."

Her eyes wandered to the darkness outside the window. We'd made it to the outskirts of the city.

"Seriously though, where the hell are you taking me?" she asked.

I gestured to the lights closing in ahead with a grin. She squinted her eyes, and her face brightened.

"A fair?" she muttered.

"Yeah, you ever been to one of these?" I parked the car in

the dirt lot of the fairgrounds a good distance from the entrance.

She rolled her eyes. "Yes, I've been to one of these. It's been a while. Probably over ten years."

"Well, now you get to experience it with me." I shot her a charming smile.

Fluorescent neon lights from the rides and booths shone brightly as we made our way up to the ticket box. I paid for the full package.

Once we were in, I asked her, "Where should we start? You wanna go on a ride or play some games?"

She smiled, and her gaze went to the milk bottle knockdown game. "How good is your throwing arm?"

"Let's find out." I stared into her eyes, forgetting where I was.

It turned out Julia had a good fucking arm on her. I lost to her twice, and she left the game booth with an overstuffed panda bear.

"You let me win, didn't you?" she asked, hugging her new prize to her chest.

"Believe it or not, I actually tried." I caught sight of the Ferris wheel. "You wanna ride that next?" I gestured toward it, and she seemed hesitant. "Unless you want to go on a different ride."

She glanced at me. "No, I'm okay with the Ferris wheel."

We waited in line for about ten minutes, and when we got to the front, the worker's eyes looked like they were going to pop out of his head.

"Oh my god, Lucas Verduce," he said, escorting us up

the platform to the two-person seat of the ride. "Oh my fucking god, I can't believe it. *The* Lucas Verduce is here."

"Yeah, that's me," I said in a low tone, and he seemed to understand that I didn't want to be found out.

"Sorry, man." He threw a glance at Julia and smiled before turning back to me. "I just have to say, I really love that new song."

"Thanks." I grinned. I loved running into fans despite the trouble it caused sometimes. "Hey, you wouldn't want some tickets to our next show, would you?"

The guy's face lit up even more—if that was possible. "Yeah, I'd love that."

He quickly tapped his information into my phone and handed it back. I told him there would be four tickets waiting for him at the box office of the venue. He shook my hand and thanked me more times than needed, but I was used to it. My fans meant a lot, and I realized that I might've taken them for granted in the past.

The ride started in silence. I'd noticed Julia limping as we walked around earlier. Hopefully the ride would give her knee a break for a little while.

She clutched the stuffed panda to her chest and peered out at the city lights in the distance. We slid closer together, our sides touching. *Maybe bringing her here wasn't such a good idea after all.* I figured we needed a breather from the interviews and parties, but I hadn't expected hanging out with her as a friend would be this fucking hard when all I wanted to do was touch her. Hold her. Kiss her.

Fuck, I need to stop.

"That was nice. What you did for that man," Julia said, still peering out into the night sky. The gentle balmy breeze stirred the free strands of her wavy hair.

"I wouldn't have gotten this far if not for my fans," I replied.

Silence ensued as she inhaled, then exhaled.

"Thank you. I needed this." Her gaze met mine.

"I did too. Honestly, I'm glad you decided to come. Don't know what I would've done otherwise."

The seat shifted. Was she leaning toward me? I turned my head to see what she was doing and caught her lips with mine.

Her eyes widened, and she pulled away, her lips curving up. "I meant to get your cheek."

I grinned. "I'm not complaining."

She looked away. "How'd you convince Ethan to let you out without a bodyguard?"

The ride jerked a little. "I have someone watching us. He's keeping his distance."

She glanced down at the passersby with a curious look on her face.

"You won't be able to see him. He's good at being invisible," I said with a grin. God, she was adorable.

Silence filled the space between us once more before I asked, "Did I do something wrong?"

"What makes you think you did something wrong?"

"I don't know. You just seem off after last night's party. I wanted to make sure I hadn't done anything to upset you."

The Ferris wheel stopped, and the workers started helping people off the ride. We lingered at the very top.

Julia bit down on her plump bottom lip. "I told you, I'm fine."

"That usually means you're not," I muttered.

"I don't know what you want me to say, Lucas."

Now I knew something had to be bothering her, and I was going to pry it out of her whether she liked it or not. "I don't know, how about the truth?"

She swallowed as the wheel turned a bit more. "It doesn't matter."

I frowned and ran a hand through my hair. "I thought we were friends?"

Her eyes had become glossy. "We are," she whispered.

"So, why can't you tell me what's wrong?" I prodded.

When we reached the platform and the worker released the bar that held us in the seat, she darted off the ride and into the crowd of people.

"Jules, wait." I followed, pushing through the sea of fairgoers.

She was fucking running from me again, pushing me away. I should've predicted this, should've expected it.

"Where the hell are you going?" I finally caught up to her.

She spun around to face me, that familiar fire in her eyes. "Why'd you have to fucking ruin this?"

"How did I ruin this? I just asked a simple question."

"Whatever. Take me back to the hotel." She turned around and headed toward the exit.

I grabbed her arm, stopping her. "No. We've only been here for an hour. We have to at least have some funnel cake. And I promise to drop it."

She stood there for a moment, studying me before she conceded. "Fine. But only because I love funnel cake."

We walked past a group of guys, and their eyes locked onto Julia. I heard them whisper " 'My Crimson Love' " and knew they recognized her. Heat ignited in my core as I placed my hand on her lower back and guided her toward a booth selling various souvenirs.

Julia turned, a questioning look on her face.

With a devious smile, I stopped, picked a woven straw cowboy hat from a nearby rack, and placed it on her head. "Here."

"I'm not wearing this," she deadpanned.

The guys were still watching her.

"I think you need a disguise."

"Why?" She looked around before her gaze landed back on me. "Fine, but you're gonna wear one too."

She immediately went for a white cowboy hat with a feathered band and plopped it on my head. We glanced at our reflection in the mirror. She definitely pulled it off better than me.

What if that's all she wore? My cock twitched against my jeans. *Down, boy.*

Her eyes narrowed as though she could read my mind, but she said nothing and continued to the checkout counter.

The rest of the evening went by quickly. We played more games, and she even shared some of her funnel cake with me. I caught her staring at me a few times and wondered if she was fighting her feelings for me. Maybe she used anger as a shield to keep people at bay. But it seemed like every time I thought I had her figured out, my assumptions were fucking wrong.

We arrived back at the hotel around midnight. My and Julia's rooms were on the same floor, so we really didn't have a choice but to head up together, still wearing those fucking cowboy hats.

"I really do appreciate tonight, Lucas. And I'm sorry I kinda snapped earlier. It's just been . . ." She pursed her lips as we walked through the modern lobby to the elevator doors. "A bit stressful lately."

I wished she would talk to me about what was bothering her, but I didn't want her to run or push me away even more. *God, she's fucking stubborn.*

"I'm just glad we got to hang out."

We stepped into the elevator, and the ride up was silent. Once we reached the fifth floor, she rushed out and headed down the hall.

I trailed behind her. "Is there a fire somewhere?"

She stopped and faced me, her brow furrowed. "Huh?"

"You just seem eager to get to your room," I said with a grin, closing the space between us.

She bit down on her bottom lip. "I'm a little tired." Her heated gaze met mine for the hundredth time that night; it was the same one that said she wanted me.

I brought my face inches from hers, testing her reaction.

"I know what you're doing, Jules. But I don't understand why you're doing it."

For a second, her gaze softened, and I could've sworn her body swayed toward me, but she stepped away, leaving me feeling like I'd imagined the whole thing. Maybe I wanted her so bad that I *had* imagined it.

"Good night. Thanks again." She turned on her heel, clutching her stuffed panda, and shuffled down the hall and into her room.

THIS IS FUCKING BULLSHIT. WAS LUCAS REALLY MELTING the icy exterior of my heart? *Utter bullshit!*

I didn't know how to handle this, how to replace those barriers I'd worked so hard on throughout the years. We were walking the fine line of friendship and lovers, and our little night out on the town had blurred it even more.

After we'd gone to that fair together, he'd made it a priority to meet in the lobby of whatever hotel we stayed at. We sat and talked about anything and everything. Most nights we wouldn't go to bed until five in the morning.

Between rehearsals and performances, I had to make appearances at parties and dinners, as usual. Through the next few weeks, Ethan scheduled interviews with the press to clear up the annoying rumors about me and Lucas dating. It turned out his fans "shipped" us, rooted for a romance between us. *Fuck that.*

In what seemed like the fucking blink of an eye, there

were only three weeks left in the tour. I would return to the studio, to my normal life *without* Lucas. There was one problem: I didn't know if I wanted that life back.

After our last show in Savannah, the crew loaded up the equipment, and we prepped to make our way to the next location in Florida. As I followed Mia and Lita up the bus steps, Kyle came out of nowhere and pulled me off, causing me to stumble and nearly bust my ass.

"What the fuck, Kyle?" I adjusted the tote on my shoulder and crossed my arms.

He ran a hand through his blond hair, a smirk on his handsome face. "You're not riding in this bus tonight, sweetheart."

I cocked an eyebrow. "Oh really? Who said?"

He gestured over his shoulder to Lucas's bus. "Who else?"

It was about a three-hour ride to Jacksonville. Wouldn't hurt to ride with the guys, right? *Maybe Lucas and I can get all our talking out of the way and actually go to bed early.*

I walked over to the sleek bus and climbed up the narrow steps. Ethan, Mark, and Billy were in the lounge area sipping on some beers.

"Well, if it isn't our lovely ballerina." Ethan raised his bottle to me. "Want a beer?"

I shook my head. "No, I'm fine, thanks."

"Lucas is waiting for you in the back room," Billy said, his eyes on the TV, which hung on the wall across from the sectional.

Mark remained his usual quiet self which I appreciated.

He seemed like a nice guy. A bit mysterious, but nice nonetheless.

"Thanks." I swallowed, alarms going off in my head, telling me to abort this mission and go back to the other bus, where it was safe. As I was about to do just that, Lucas poked his head out of the back room and called my name. The movement of the bus caused me to lose my balance. I caught myself on the railing.

Too late to turn back now. I inhaled, then blew it out, padding through the lounge and down the narrow hallway into the room.

Lucas sat on the king-size bed in nothing but his black basketball shorts, his guitar in his lap. It had been a while since I'd seen him shirtless, and it still affected me like it was the first time. His dark eyes locked onto me, a smirk pulling at his lips.

"Close the door and sit down," he said.

Fuck. I didn't want to do it, but my mind and body were at a constant battle with each other. It was beginning to wear me down. I climbed onto the bed and sat against the headboard, which was basically the wall, my legs stretched out in front of me. Thankfully, I'd decided to wear comfortable clothes: baggy black joggers and a tee. I kicked off my sneakers and put them on the floor next to the bed.

It was about nine in the evening, and according to the navigation on my cell, we would arrive in Jacksonville at about midnight.

Lucas and I sat there in comfortable silence as the bus shook from hitting rough areas on the highway. He strummed his guitar, stopped, and wrote something on the notepad in front of him.

"Mind if I take a peek?" I asked, fiddling my thumbs.

"Huh?" He didn't look at me as he continued to jot words down.

With a grin, I leaned forward, snatching the notepad from him before rushing off the bed and locking myself in the small adjacent bathroom.

"Seriously, Jules?" His voice dripped with irritation as he banged on the door. "You know I can break this door down, right?"

He probably could, but I said nothing. I read the words on the notepad.

She's the one I can't stop thinking about, embedded in my soul. She makes me feel, makes me mad, makes me question life. Why is she so untouchable? Why is she so perfectly lovable? I want to give her my heart, but I'm afraid she'll tear it apart.

I swallowed the lump in my throat, hands shaking. This couldn't be about me. It had to be about someone else.

"Who's this about, Lucas?" My voice trembled with the question.

"Do I really have to say?"

"Just answer the damn question," I demanded. The nervousness in my tone had faded away and turned into something I was familiar and comfortable with: anger.

"Come out and I'll tell you."

"Tell me and I'll come out."

"Why are you being so difficult right now?"

Yup, he's annoyed. Good. "Why can't you answer the question?" I asked.

The guys had turned the volume of the TV up in the lounge. It sounded like they were watching a basketball game. I sat there on the toilet seat lid, waiting for Lucas to say something. Anything.

"Fuck," he whispered. "I can't do this anymore."

I tilted my head even though he couldn't see me. "Can't do what anymore?"

"This."

"Be more specific." I was getting tired of his vagueness.

"This fucking friends thing." He raised his voice.

"Wait, what are you saying?" I stood and yanked the door open, and I stared into his hooded russet eyes. "You can't be friends with me?"

He studied me, that familiar intensity in his gaze. "No. That's not what I'm fucking saying." He ran his fingers through his dark hair. "It's really hard for me to be around you when all I want to do is touch you. When all I want to do is feel your lips against mine."

We'd been doing well. I'd thought I had him all figured out. But maybe I was just an unobservant idiot . . . or in denial. Swallowing the lump rising in my throat, I asked, "Why're you acting like this all of a sudden?"

He drew closer, drowning me in his woodsy scent. "Are you kidding me? This isn't all of a fucking sudden, Jules.

This has been happening for weeks now. You're just too fucking stubborn to admit it."

My nostrils flared, chest tightening. "I'm not doing this." I needed to get out of that room. I attempted to push past him, but he grabbed my forearm.

"We're not done," he gritted out. "God, why do you always fucking run from me?"

I yanked my arm from his grasp. "I don't—"

"Yes, you do, and it's goddamn tiring."

"Then give up." I crossed my arms.

He leaned in and pressed his forehead to mine. "Is that really what you want?"

My mind told me yes, to rid myself of any and all thoughts of this man. My heart, on the other hand, wanted everything to do with Lucas Verduce, despite knowing he could fucking destroy me.

"I've seen the way you look at me. You want this as much as I do." He gripped my waist, pulling me flush against him.

This isn't happening. I was mad at him for backing me into a corner and mad at myself for trusting him to honor our boundaries. But most of all, I was angry I'd let him into my life and my heart. "I can't fucking trust you, Lucas."

He faltered, an unreadable look on his face. "What?"

"I can't trust you." I hugged myself.

"Did I do something to make you feel that way?" He pinched his lips together.

I averted my gaze before saying, "Remember when we had that incident in the bathroom?"

He nodded, hands resting low on his hips.

"It didn't take you long to find another piece of ass to fuck." My voice was thick with resentment.

His eyes narrowed. "The fuck you talking about?"

"I ran into one of your groupies at the Beacon Theatre."

He stared at me for a moment, and then realization washed over his face as he tilted his head toward the ceiling, letting out a breath. "Fucking Laiyla."

I scoffed. "Is that her name?"

"What did she tell you?" His dark gaze bored into me.

"She said you'd been fucking her *hard*." This was stupid. I should've been content with being a one-night stand. "You know what? It doesn't fucking matter."

"It obviously does, or you wouldn't have brought it up." His voice rose.

I shifted backward until I hit the wall.

"She was lying to you, Jules." His features softened.

My muscles relaxed at his words, but I still couldn't believe him. "Even if she was, how am I supposed to believe you'd give that life up?"

His Adam's apple bobbed before he said, "Because I don't want that life anymore, Sunshine." His dark gaze invaded my soul. I couldn't look away even if I'd wanted to. "I want *you*."

My eyebrows came together. "And I'm supposed to believe that?"

He nodded, closing the distance between us. "I think you've always known the truth." He placed his hands against the wall, caging me in.

His breath was hot on my cheek as I whispered, "Don't

be so sure." I knew if I looked at him, he would kiss me, and I would let him, and I didn't know if my heart could take it.

"Look at me, Sunshine," he rasped, voice deep and full of need.

"No." It didn't come out as firm as I'd intended. This was Lucas Verduce. What could I offer him? A flooded studio? My small apartment, which I didn't even own? My broken, scarred body? Even if we did try this, it wouldn't be long until he left me, like everyone else in my life.

Fuck. My eyes blurred with tears. The barriers of my heart fractured with each drop that fell down my cheeks. I couldn't let him see me like this. Exposed. Vulnerable.

"Get away from me, Lucas." My voice trembled with each word.

"Please. Just look at me." The gentle sincerity in his tone caused me to blink up at him, tears spilling from my eyes. "You don't always have to act so tough, you know."

"I can't be what you want, Lucas," I blurted without thinking.

He shrugged. "Maybe not. But you're definitely what I *need*, Jules."

He brushed his thumb across my wet cheek, and then that same hand slid to my nape, and he pressed his lips to mine. My eyes fluttered shut as I surrendered to him. With my heart pounding against my rib cage, I circled my arms around his neck. His chest heaved with anticipation. He snaked an arm around my waist, pulling me against him.

I gasped at his warm hand reaching beneath my baggy tee, roaming my sensitive skin, all the way up to one of my breasts. He lifted the elastic of my sports bra and massaged. Reaching down, I rubbed his arousal through the threads of his basketball shorts. A guttural moan rumbled in his chest.

"Fuck," he breathed, reaching for the door and locking it.

I didn't think. Couldn't think. Primal instincts took over as I sat on the bed and grabbed his arm. When his waist was in front of me, I pulled his shorts and boxers down. His dick sprang free from its confines, and my mouth watered at the sight of it. I peered at him. His lust-filled gaze met mine, and in one slow motion, I took him into my mouth, swallowing as much of him as I could. His dick tickled my throat, but I was determined to take him *all* to the hilt.

"Fucking hell," he moaned.

I continued to pump my mouth full of him, gliding my wet lips up and down his thick shaft. My eyes wandered to his once more. He licked his lip ring, watching me suck and swallow. The walls of my pussy pulsed, begging for attention. I reached beneath the waistband of my sweats and fingered myself. A breathy noise escaped me.

"Fuck, I'm gonna come if you keep doing that," he warned.

I didn't stop until he pulled me off and pushed me back onto the bed, nearly ripping my joggers and panties off. A small squeal escaped me as he lay on his stomach and settled between my legs.

His tongue worked in circles around my already-throbbing clit.

"Shit," I hissed, drawing out the word.

He slid his index finger up and down my slit before

pushing into me. My back arched, another sound of pleasure escaping me. He penetrated my pussy with another finger, stretching me. My walls were already pulsing near orgasm.

"Lucas," I moaned as he fucked me with his fingers. The combination of his tongue and fingers sent me over the threshold. My legs trembled as I came.

He wasted no time in walking over to one of the drawers in the closet, taking out a condom, and sheathing his hard length. He pulled me to the edge of the bed, studying me while lining himself up with my entrance.

When he slid into me, my breath hitched, and my eyes rolled back.

He caressed my lips, and I captured his groan with my mouth. He worked his hips against mine. Slow. Steady. His length stroked everywhere inside me.

This wasn't at all like the sex we'd had in the bathroom. He was taking his time, making sure I was comfortable. He thrust into me harder. Faster. His fingers worked my clit as he fucked me, and before I knew it, he'd pushed me over the edge into ecstasy.

"Fuck." I covered my mouth to muffle my cries.

He traced kisses along my jawline, still pumping in and out of me. "I've missed fucking this tight pussy." His mouth went to my neck as he pinned my legs to the bed by the backs of my knees. The position allowed him to stroke into me deeper. He held nothing back after that. I was almost certain we were rocking the moving bus.

"Fuck, Lucas. So fucking deep." I dragged my fingernails down his back.

His hips slapped against mine. He drove into me hard. "God. Dammit." He grunted into the side of my neck.

I bit down on my bottom lip before he captured them, fucking me into another mind-numbing orgasm.

"Fuck, Jules, I'm so fucking close." Not long after, his abs flexed, and with one last thrust, his dick pulsed inside my throbbing pussy, spilling into the latex. He collapsed on top of me, releasing my legs.

Oh. My. Fucking. God. I didn't think I could walk. Had he actually fucked me until I couldn't walk?

He rolled off, lay next to me, and stared at the ceiling.

What was he thinking? What was I thinking? All I knew was that was the most intense sex I'd ever had. What had I expected though? I was sure he'd had plenty of practice. Despite all that, I still fucking wanted him. Why was this all so confusing?

He turned and propped himself up on his hand. "So . . . there's something else."

What else could there be? He'd gotten what he wanted. *Again.* I sat up and climbed off the bed, looking for my underwear and pants. After I threw his boxers and shorts at him, I walked into the small adjacent bathroom to clean up.

"You okay, Sunshine?" he asked as I washed my hands in the sink.

"Yeah, just tired," I lied, walking out of the bathroom.

He was sitting up with his legs over the edge of the bed. "Come here." He held out a hand.

He looked so determined and focused. What was he going to say?

I padded over and took his hand, and he reached for my other one. His head tilted upward, russet eyes locking onto mine.

"This may or may not come as a surprise to you." He looked away for a moment, inhaling a deep breath. "But I'm—"

There was a loud knock on the door. "Hey, fuckers, we're about thirty minutes from the hotel, so finish up. I also gotta take a major piss." It was Billy.

I released a sigh, relieved by the interruption.

"Fuck," Lucas said, walking over to the door to let the drummer in.

"Jesus! Smells like sex in here," Billy said as he made the short walk to the bathroom, slamming the door shut.

I didn't say anything to Lucas, just made my way out to the lounge area and sat between Ethan and Mark as if nothing had happened. What was Lucas going to tell me? It could've been anything.

Whatever, the moment had passed. I decided that our little fuck session was nothing more than another moment of weakness.

Yeah, weakness . . .

I was about to tell her, but fucking Billy had to interrupt us like the piece of shit he was. God, why couldn't I tell her how I felt? Why was it so hard to get three little words out of my fucking mouth? It didn't make any sense. I could perform in front of thousands of people, yet I was a complete dumbfuck about my own feelings.

If I'd known Julia was going to avoid me like the fucking plague once we arrived in Jacksonville, I would've just blurted it out on the bus. I should've expected this from her, should've expected her to push me away. *Again.* It seemed to happen every time we had sex.

Fuck . . . I should've given up, but my stupid heart wouldn't let me. How could I prove to her that I wasn't the man the media made me out to be? How could I prove to her that I wasn't going anywhere?

The days leading up to our first show in Jacksonville

were packed with interviews, dinners, parties, and rehearsals. Didn't help that the label was based out of Florida. It seemed like they were keeping us extra busy. I was so glad our contract ended soon.

Thousands of people had gathered in the arena. The crowd went crazy as we played some of our past hits. I sang a cover of a song by Maroon 5, turning the ladies to Jell-O. Soon, it was time to end the concert with "My Crimson Love." Julia danced on the stage in her usual black leotard, skirt wrap, and pointe shoes. Even though the dance had been choreographed, she'd made it her own. The grace and ease of her movements never ceased to amaze me.

Toward the end of the song, during the chorus, I placed my guitar on its stand while singing, then walked up to Julia and serenaded her. She shot me a look of confusion. It wasn't part of the routine, but I ignored her with a grin and kept singing.

When the song ended, I grabbed her by the waist, pulled her against me, and kissed her in front of the packed arena. The crowd roared. It was a deafening sound, like the crashing of waves against a shore. People were cheering, chanting, and clapping. The lights dimmed, and she pushed me away with wide eyes. She brought her fingers to her lips and turned, running off the stage. I ran after her.

She sprinted down one of the tunnels toward the buses.

"Julia." I called her name multiple times. She ignored me, as expected. Finally, I caught up to her and blocked her path. "Would you stop and talk to me, Jules?"

Her nostrils flared. Fuck, she wasn't happy.

"Talk to you? How about what the fuck, Lucas? What made you think it was okay to do that?"

I stuffed my hands into my pockets. "I don't know, felt right at the time."

"Do you know how much shit you're gonna have to deal with? No. Better yet, all the shit *I'm* gonna have to deal with?" She threw her hands up. "I can't believe you. All the work put into making them think we're friends just went down the drain."

The cheers of the audience had died down by then as I stared at her.

This is it. I had to tell her.

"I love you." It came out like word vomit, not as eloquent as I'd wanted it to be.

She froze and stared at me, an unreadable expression on her face. What the hell was she thinking? Did she expect me to say more?

"Did you hear what I said?" I stepped closer. "I love you, Sunshine."

A few torturous seconds passed before she asked, "Why?"

I stared at her for a moment. "What?"

"Why?"

This woman is maddening.

I crept toward her. "I don't know. How do you expect me to explain something like this?"

She let out a slow breath before saying, "Try."

Performing in front of thousands of people was easy compared to what she was asking me to do. I needed to find my words. My eyes locked onto hers.

"You're fearless in everything you do. Dancing and life in general. You're not afraid to tell me to fuck off." That earned me a smirk from her. "The passion you have for dance reminded me why I love music. Hell, I even started writing lyrics again. I found my purpose, but that doesn't mean shit without you. I love you, and I don't care who hears." My voice was thick with all the emotions of the evening. "I want the entire universe to know that I love you, Julia Blackwell."

I put it all out there for her to digest, holding nothing back. She gazed at me, her lips pursed, arms crossed. With the muffled sound of the crowd and my heart racing in my ears, I waited.

Just as she opened her mouth to speak, Ethan jogged up to us, brow furrowed, taking deep breaths. "Luc, what the fuck are you doing? Do you know what you just did?"

"Not right now, man—"

He stood between me and Julia. "Oh yes, fucking now. You have to go out there and deal with the mess you made."

Fuck, he was right. I had to say something to the press, or they would eat Julia alive. She tore her gaze away from mine and started toward the buses. My heart sank into my stomach at the sight of her getting farther and farther away from me. Did this mean she didn't feel the same?

"Let's go." Ethan led me in the opposite direction.

Dammit, what had I done? I probably should've just talked to her about it, but it really had seemed like a good idea at the time. I hadn't known she'd be angry at me for it.

How was I going to fix this fucking mess? And better yet, how was I going to confront Julia?

CHAPTER 22

Julia

I NEEDED TO GET THE FUCK OUT OF THERE. LUCAS fucking Verduce had admitted he loved me. And the worst part of the whole thing was I'd said nothing. *Nothing*. My brain had lost the ability to form fucking words. What would I have said though? Knowing me, I probably would've just responded in anger.

Mia ran up to me as I neared the buses. "Jules, oh my god. What just happened?"

I dragged my palms down my face and covered my mouth. *He didn't mean it. Couldn't have meant it.* My heart pounded in my chest, and for a moment, I thought my head would explode.

"Are you okay?" she asked. "You wanna go somewhere?"

"Fuck yeah." I changed out of my stage clothes and into comfortable loungewear. It was about eleven at night, but I didn't care. Mia and I made the short trek to St. Johns River.

One of the security guys trailed us. He stayed out of earshot, giving us privacy.

We walked along the riverfront as the lights from the buildings across the way reflected off the water. A gentle balmy breeze wisped through my long onyx hair as Lucas's words repeated over and over in my head. *I love you.* I stopped and stared into the distance.

"What happened, Jules?" Mia walked up beside me. "Besides that kiss."

I shook my head, swallowing the lump in my throat.

"Okay. I guess I'll go first, then." She took a deep breath. "I think I've pretty much fallen for Kyle."

My eyes widened, and I faced her. "Oh my god, Mia."

I knew they'd been spending a lot of time together. Guess I'd been too consumed in Lucas to notice just how much. A wave of guilt washed over me.

She seemed to notice my remorseful tone. "No. It's fine. You seemed really happy with Lucas."

I didn't want to admit it, but all those sleepless nights spent talking to him were the happiest I'd had been in a while. "Have you told Kyle?" I asked.

"No. Truth is, I'm not sure if he feels the same," she replied.

I nodded, and the peaceful sound of flowing water filled the silence between us. Being near any body of water always calmed my nerves.

"So, what happened?" she prodded.

Upon my exhale, I said, "He told me he loves me."

She stared at me for a long moment. "This is Lucas Verduce we're talking about, right?"

"Yeah, I know. Shocker." I grinned.

"No. Not really."

What did she mean by that?

"Explain." I crossed my arms.

The corner of her mouth rose. "I mean, it was only a matter of time before he completely fell head over heels for you."

"Yeah, but that doesn't mean anything. Our lifestyles are so different."

She let out a sharp breath. "You're using that as an excuse."

No, I wasn't. "How do you figure?"

A severe look crossed her face. "It's always something with you. Your relationship with Derek ended because he didn't like cats, and you don't even have one. Hardly a deal-breaker, Jules."

My eyebrows came together. "It wasn't just that. He couldn't accept the fact that I put my career first."

"My point is you always find a reason why it won't work. And you don't pay attention to the reasons it could work," she said, staring me dead in the eyes. The moon shone high above us, giving the water an otherworldly shimmer. "Honestly, I don't know why you're so afraid to take a chance with him."

Fuck. Maybe she was right. Maybe I'd overreacted a tad bit. Maybe I should've considered how I felt for a moment instead of ignoring it or responding in anger. Like I always did. "Come on, we should get back."

Thirty minutes passed before we made it to the venue. We neared Lucas's bus.

Why the fuck is it rocking? Muffled grunts and moans came from inside. *Oh, hell no.* My heart dropped into my stomach as I approached, debating whether I should go in or not.

"Who do you think it is?" That same worry filled Mia's eyes.

I let out a sharp breath and didn't respond. As I opened the door and climbed up the three steps of the bus, the moans became louder. *It better be Billy, Mark, or Lita getting some.*

Mia waited at the bottom of the steps, dread apparent on her tan face.

God, those fucking sex sounds were obnoxious. I made my way through the lounge to the back room. Tiptoed up to the door and grabbed the chrome knob, but before I turned it, I took a deep breath. On my exhale, I pushed the door open. My hands flew over my mouth as realization hit me like a ton of bricks.

"Kyle?" I shouted.

He rolled off the bed butt-ass naked. The girl he'd been having sex with was that same one from the concert, Laiyla.

Fucking bitch.

Next thing I knew, Mia charged into the room with tears pouring down her cheeks. She lunged at Kyle, but I blocked her path and held her back. Was it fucked-up that I was relieved it was Kyle and not Lucas?

"You fucking asshole. I should've known you'd fucking do this, you piece of shit," she shrieked, her voice shaking with each word.

After what she'd told me on our walk, her reaction was so fucking warranted. Kyle had just shattered her heart, and he didn't even look remorseful about it. How did I know Lucas wouldn't do the same to me? Both men were accustomed to the same lifestyle and had similar track records when it came to women.

"Mia, I can explain," he tried to say.

I wrapped my arms around my best friend to keep her from hurting herself and him.

"I don't wanna fucking hear it." She buried her face in my shoulder and sobbed, soaking my loose black tee. I didn't care, but I needed to get her the fuck out of there.

Laiyla lay on the bed with a smug grin, and it took everything in me not to slap it off her stupid fucking face. Instead, I turned to Kyle as he pulled on some shorts, covering his junk. "You just lost the best thing that has ever happened to you. I can *guarantee* you'll regret this for the rest of your pathetic life." Then I walked off the bus, leading a sobbing Mia along with me.

Fuck. Was that going to be my future with Lucas if I gave him a chance? My heart shattered for Mia, and I realized . . . I couldn't do this anymore. Couldn't continue the tour. Couldn't put my heart on the line. The money wasn't worth this bullshit. I didn't waste another second and packed my and Mia's things.

The cab pulled up to the curb, and before I climbed in, I took one last glance at the parked tour buses. *Goodbye, Lucas Verduce.*

Lucas

THE PRESS BOUGHT THE VAGUE ANSWERS I'D GIVEN them. They were satiated for the moment. I made my way through the tunnel to the buses, but something felt off. The security personnel appeared to be searching for something or someone. My heart sank into my stomach. *She wouldn't . . .*

Ethan strode up to me. "We have a situation."

The blood rushed from my head to my heart, increasing my pulse.

"What happened?" I bit out.

"She's gone. Both of them. They left without saying a word to anyone."

I knew Ethan and Mia had become friends, but I hadn't realized how close they were until I saw that look in his eyes, a look I was all too familiar with.

Why would they fucking leave like that? Why would *she* leave? Was it my confession? I ran my fingers through my hair before my hand made a fist. "Does anyone know why?"

At that moment, Kyle and Laiyla walked off the bus holding hands, and I knew it had something to do with them.

"Mia and Julia caught Kyle and Laiyla in the back of the bus, if you know what I mean," Ethan said as I stared daggers at Kyle.

That motherfucker. My legs moved beneath me.

"Luc, don't. He's not worth it." Ethan trailed behind me.

"What the fuck did you do, Kyle?" I lunged, shoving Kyle against the bus. Laiyla squeaked, covering her mouth.

Kyle frowned. "The fuck you talking about?"

"Is it true Mia and Julia caught you two fucking?" I was trying my best to keep my voice calm.

He straightened. "Yeah, so what?"

I knew Mia was developing strong feelings for Kyle. She might have even fallen for him from what Julia had told me. "Mia really fucking liked you, man. How could you do that to her?"

"Dude, what're you talking about? You act like you've never done this before." Kyle genuinely thought he'd done nothing wrong, and it pissed me off.

"That was before I met Julia, and you fucking up with Mia may have ruined my chances," I said. "Thanks a lot, asshole."

Ethan stood by with two security guys. I didn't blame him.

"What's so special about that bitch anyway? It's just pussy." A smirk crept onto Kyle's face as he crossed his arms.

I clenched my fist and, without thinking, punched Kyle square in the jaw. He twisted from the impact as Laiyla let out a scream. Ethan grabbed me before I could throw another swing.

"Fuck you, Kyle," I spat. "Get her the fuck out of here, Ethan. I don't want to see her fucking face for the rest of the tour."

My best friend held me back while Laiyla slipped past us with one of the security guards, her eyes full of tears. I didn't fucking care. Julia was gone. She was *gone*.

Kyle attempted to hit me, but the other guard stepped in and held him back.

"What is it with you? You've fucking changed," he said, struggling against the large man.

"Walk away." Ethan turned me away and pushed me about twenty feet from the scene.

He let me go, and I immediately pulled out my phone. I called Julia, but it went straight to voicemail. After trying a few more times, I knew she turned off her cell.

"Fuck!" I headed toward the gate of the enclosed parking area.

"Wait, where the hell you going?" Ethan stopped me at the chain-link fence, blocking my path.

"I'm getting the fuck out of here." I pocketed my phone. "I'm done, Ethan. Done with *everything*." A lump formed in my throat.

He studied me and took a step closer. "What about the tour? You have a few more shows."

I didn't say anything, just shook my head, pulse ringing in my ears.

"What's so special about her, Luc? You have a plethora of women to choose from." His eyebrows came together.

Of course he didn't understand. Ethan no longer believed there was only one person out there for him. I'd had the same mindset until Julia came along.

"I don't fucking care." My voice lowered. "I just want one. I want *her*. And she's gone."

"What about your fans? And the label? You gonna throw all that away for some chick?" Ethan asked, standing between me and the gate. Two security guards approached us, but Ethan told them he had the situation under control, and they backed off.

"She's not just some chick, Ethan, and I need you to fucking get that." My heart pounded in my chest. "Fuck." I paced over to the cement wall of the tunnel, completely losing myself in thought. What if this was it? What if I'd lost her for good? I should've told her how I truly felt in the beginning instead of enticing her with a fucking contract.

Ethan stepped closer and placed a heavy hand on my shoulder. "Finish the tour. You have less than three weeks. Then you can go find her. This isn't just about you, man. There are a lot of people involved, and if you leave, it could cause a hell of a chain reaction."

Shit. He was fucking right. I couldn't leave no matter how bad I wanted to. I was the lead singer. Lead guitarist. The face of No Blood, No Alibi.

With a nod, I inhaled, flicking my lip ring with my tongue. "I'll finish the tour, but you need to keep Kyle the fuck away from me. I only wanna see him onstage, and that's it."

He agreed. "I'll stick him in Lita's bus when we're on the road."

In my solitude, thoughts of losing Julia plagued me. I wondered if she thought I'd do the same thing Kyle had done to Mia. She had to know I wouldn't do that. Sure, we had certain things in common, but he was more of a fuckboy than I could ever be—it just wasn't publicized. The media misconstrued a lot about me, but I'd never cared, because I knew I wasn't the person they made me out to be.

The three weeks went by so fucking slow, I thought my heart was going to spontaneously combust. I missed my and Julia's late-night talks. Her sweet, condescending voice. The way she laughed at my jokes. The way her brow furrowed whenever something I'd said confused her. The way she bit her lip when she was in deep thought. Her silky skin against mine when I'd made love to her. *Fuck . . .*

That floral scent of hers haunted my senses. Julia Blackwell was it for me, and I didn't know what I'd do if I couldn't have her.

CHAPTER 24

Julia

The only place I could think of that the paparazzi didn't know about was my dad's house in the suburbs near NYC. This was the house I had spent most of my teenage years in. Hell, my old room looked exactly how I'd left it. There were still posters of my favorite rock bands on the walls. Dance trophies sat on the old white dresser, and my burgundy comforter decorated the full-size bed.

It had been one week since Mia and I had left the tour. I'd turned our phones off, so the only way anyone could think to get ahold of us was through my dad, but he had no idea what was going on, just that we needed a place to stay.

Mia was so fucking wrecked over that douche, and I wasn't going to be an asshole about it by telling her "I told you so." To be honest, I'd let my *own* guard down around Lucas, and if Kyle hadn't fucked Mia over, I would've fallen completely.

Everything happens for a reason . . . right?

My heart broke having to pick up the pieces of Mia's as the days passed. There were times I had to force her to eat and shower. I wished there were something I could do to take the pain away, but it would take time.

I should've slugged that asshole when I had the chance.

Dad never once asked me what had happened. I didn't know what he thought. Did he even care? Maybe he was giving me space. I had no idea where I would start if he asked.

After dinner one night, I helped Dad wash dishes in the small kitchen. The window above the double-basin sink gave me a panoramic view of the green backyard. I caught myself daydreaming a few times. My eyes were dry from getting no sleep; that was partially Mia's fault. She would cry herself to sleep some nights. I let out a breath and leaned against the porcelain sink for a minute.

Dad glanced at me like he wanted to say something. He soaped up the dishes while I dried them and put them away.

"Just ask." I dried a plate before placing it in the white cabinet next to the sink.

He looked at the dish in his hand, wiping it down with the sudsy yellow sponge. "It's none of my business."

"But?"

"You broke your contract, Jay Bird. I don't think you realize how serious that is," he said.

I glanced at my hands. "I do, Pops, believe me. Everything was too fucked-up to ride out. I think I left just in time."

"In time?" He studied me for a second. "For what?"

Fuck.

Lucas's confession came flooding back. His russet eyes had focused on me like I was the only person who mattered to him. Then he'd said it, the three words I never thought I'd hear from him. *I love you.*

My chest constricted like it was going to cave in, and my cheeks warmed as I stepped away from the sink.

Dad stopped washing dishes and dried his hands, waiting for me to respond.

"The same fucking thing would've happened to me if I'd stayed," I blurted, then realized how crazy I must have sounded to him.

A look of concern crossed his face. He took my hands and gently squeezed. "What the hell happened, Jay Bird? Did he hurt you?"

I shook my head, swallowing the lump in my throat. "No."

"What, then?" His brow furrowed.

"Mia fell for Kyle, who we caught fucking another girl in the back of the tour bus," I explained, glancing at my bare feet.

Dad still appeared confused. "What's that got to do with you?"

Fuck. He was going to make me say it. "I know it's stupid and absurd and you've warned me about you musician types . . ." Tears welled up in my eyes, and I couldn't believe I was admitting it. "But I was falling for Lucas."

He let go of my hands. "You 'were' falling, or you 'have' fallen for him?"

I shrugged and faced the sink, leaning against it.

"I think you do know. This could be a good thing." He stepped toward me.

"No, it's fucking not, Pops. This is the exact opposite."

He crossed his arms. "Explain."

My heart ached as I inhaled a breath, then exhaled. Explain? What was there to explain? There was *nothing* to fucking explain. Tears blurred my vision, but I wasn't crying. Not yet, anyway.

"It was only a matter of time before he hurt me too." I bit down on my bottom lip, blinking back the emotions that surfaced. This wasn't me. I had never been so torn and in my feelings before.

What the fuck did he do to me?

"Is that what you think?" Mia stood in the doorway of the kitchen. Her hair was twisted up in a blue towel. She'd just stepped out of the shower and was already dressed in her unicorn-print pajamas.

I sighed and faced her. "He's in that type of lifestyle, Mia."

She clasped her hands together and looked at the laminate floor. "Kyle isn't Lucas, Jules. Not even close."

With a frown, I sighed. "I know that."

"Do you though?" She stared at me. Her dark brown eyes were puffy and red from crying. Remnants of her heartbreak still glistened in them. "Kyle *never* looked at me the way Lucas looks at you."

"I doubt that." Where was the resentment? The anger? I didn't want to believe what she was telling me.

"Are you really that stupid? Lucas only ever had eyes for you. When Kyle and I were seeing each other, he told me how Lucas would go home early from partying. How he quit sleeping with groupies. Kyle told me how utterly lovesick Lucas was for you." Mia stepped closer. "I would've done anything to have Kyle look at me the way Lucas looks at you." A tear trickled down her tan cheek.

My mind flashed back to all the times Lucas had stared at me, to our first scene on set at the music video shoot. On tour, he'd smiled and winked at me during almost every performance. When he signed autographs after, he hadn't shown interest in any of the women wanting to have their ass or tits signed. She was right.

She's fucking right. I'd been so fucking blind. My hands trembled as I hugged myself. "Why didn't you say anything?" It came out as a whisper.

"Would it have mattered?" Her brows came together, lips forming a straight line. "You're so fucking stubborn and scared. You were set on the Lucas the media portrayed. You didn't even give him the benefit of the doubt."

Fucking hell. My thoughts spun in circles as nausea set in. It became difficult for me to breathe. I sprinted out of the kitchen, past the living room, and through the front door before collapsing onto the freshly cut grass in the small front yard.

Lucas had tried so hard to prove himself to me, and I'd shut him down every time. He'd wanted to give me his heart, but I'd been too fucking afraid to take it, too fucking afraid to take a chance and give him mine. Why did loving someone have to hurt this much?

Weeks of suppressed emotion came pouring out of my eyes. My shoulders shook as I covered my face with my hands and sobbed. Dad walked out shortly after with the calmest, most compassionate look on his face. He crouched down and embraced me without a word. My tears soaked the sleeve of his shirt.

I'd been so stupid in assuming that Lucas was who the media portrayed him to be. Our nightly conversations had proven he wasn't that person at all. It was probably too late to make things right between us.

I'd lost him.

Another week passed, and I realized it was the last week of the tour. No one had tried to get ahold of us. I'd stopped by the studio a few times to confirm it was still being worked on. I only hoped none of my students' parents were trying to get ahold of me.

In Your Head had a few gigs that week. Dad had invited us out, but we'd decided to stay in; Mia wasn't quite ready to go out. We sat in the living room watching TV, and I absent-mindedly scrolled through social media on my tablet. One of those blind-date reality shows played in the background. A few minutes passed before Mia changed it to live coverage of No Blood, No Alibi's last concert in Miami, Florida.

Why does she want to watch them? Is she a masochist?

"Do we have to watch this?" I whined.

She glanced at me, a grin on her face. "No better way to get over someone, right?"

With a huff, I replied, "I guess."

Even through my dad's large flat-screen TV, my heart fractured at the sight of Lucas. It must have been the high definition making him appear hotter than usual. How could I be in love with someone I wanted to throat punch occasionally? But lately, I just wanted to love him.

The camera zoomed in on Kyle shredding on his electric guitar, and Mia threw popcorn at the screen. "Boo . . ."

I chuckled. She seemed to be in better spirits.

"Lucas looks hot tonight," she said, a corner of her mouth rising.

Not what I needed to hear, but okay.

They usually played "My Crimson Love" as the last song of the night, but they didn't. Lucas wiped the sweat off his forehead with the bottom of his black tee before he spoke into the mic in front of him. After he thanked the fans for supporting the band, he said, "Tonight will be my last performance. I've decided to retire."

Mia's eyes widened along with mine.

There was an uproar from the audience in the huge stadium. It was easily the largest crowd they'd performed in front of, not including the people watching from home.

Lucas said, "It's been an experience, to say the least. But I'm ready to start a next chapter in my life."

Alarms went off in my head, and my heart skipped a fucking beat.

"Oh my god," Mia squealed, sitting straight up from the cappuccino suede couch.

I shushed her as I stood, snatching the remote and raising the volume of the TV.

"This last song was inspired by someone very special. She has challenged me from the first day we met and has taught me a lot about myself. It's called 'Sunshine and Madness.' " Lucas counted the band in, and they accompanied him as he sang the lyrics to the song.

I stared at the screen like a fucking mindless idiot, trying to comprehend everything.

"Jules, you okay? You're not having a stroke, are you?" Mia waved a hand in front of my face, snapping me out of my trance.

"I-I'm fine." I continued listening to the lyrics of the song as memories came surging back: How he'd thrown his drink on me when we first met, only for me to throw coffee on him the next day. The music video and teaching him how to dance. Our many arguments. Our conversations about life.

It all overwhelmed me to a point where I had to remind myself to breathe.

The last line of the song had me completely floored: *You came into my life, knocked me off its axis, I want you to know, you're the sunshine to my madness.*

"Holy shit," Mia muttered.

"What?"

"If that isn't a proclamation of love, I don't know what is," she said, hugging her knees to her chest.

I continued to stand there. "What should I do? Should I call him?"

She shot me a severe look. "Really, bitch? You're gonna call him after all that? He'll probably be swamped with interviews and events until he gets back to New York."

"Okay?" What the hell did she expect me to do? Wait at his penthouse like some stalker?

"He probably won't be home until the middle of next week. Even then, he'll probably have a shit ton of interviews. You should wait a bit," she said with a shrug as if it were the most logical thing to do.

I didn't want to admit it, but she was right, again. I couldn't talk to him about this over the phone. That was too impersonal. So, even though I had to wait another week or two, I decided to face him and tell him I was sorry for being such a coward. Admit how stupid I was for not seeing his willingness to commit and apologize for judging him by his past. For not accepting the person he was becoming—or more like the person he was *trying* to become. I hadn't given him a chance to be that person. Just thinking about it made me sick to my fucking stomach.

Mia decided that weekend she was ready to get back to life. We caught a cab to her apartment and dropped her off before I headed to mine. Great. She'd left me alone with my fucking thoughts.

I stared at the phone in my hand. I pressed the power button, and the screen lit up. No important voicemails or texts from my students' parents. *Good.* There weren't any from Lucas or Ethan either, which was surprising. I'd broken the contract. Unless . . .

Had Lucas created the contract to get close to me? If that was the case, I was a fucking idiot. Mentally, I slapped myself in the face.

The week didn't pass as fast as I wanted it to, especially with me not having my ballet studio up and running. It left me with plenty of time to reconsider my decision to confess my feelings to Lucas. I was going to risk being rejected by him, though he had proclaimed his love for me on national television. Kind of? Honestly, I didn't know what to expect. It was my own personal hell.

I decided to catch a taxi to Lucas's apartment building on Saturday. I texted Ethan to see if Lucas was busy. From reading his messages, he didn't seem all that happy with me. I didn't blame him.

ETHAN

He's at home right now.

ME

Thanks. I really appreciate it.

ETHAN

You really cut him deep when you left.

ME

I'm sorry.

I didn't know how else to respond to that.

ETHAN

Don't tell me that.

The ride there seemed short despite the traffic. *Do I really want to do this?* Before I knew it, I stood in front of the tall sleek apartment building, my hands shaking, heart thrumming in my chest. Fuck, I needed to walk inside before the urge to run away became stronger.

Willing my legs to move beneath me, I made my way up to the reception desk.

A dark-haired woman dressed in a black suit and tie asked, "What can I do for you, ma'am?"

"Uh." I placed my forearms on the desk and tapped the smooth surface with my index finger. "Lucas Verduce in today?"

The receptionist glanced at my hand.

"Sorry." I immediately stopped. "Nervous habit." *Fuck.* Hopefully I wouldn't embarrass myself and vomit, because I definitely felt nauseous.

She picked up the phone and dialed a few numbers on the keypad. "Mr. Verduce, I have a visitor, Miss . . ."

"B-Blackwell, Julia," I stuttered.

There was a suspicious look on her face as she spoke on the phone. She probably thought I was some groupie or something. It didn't help that I probably didn't look my best. I'd been sleeping like shit and hardly eating anything.

What's taking so long? Then I wondered if he'd moved on, if he had some chick up there keeping him company. Blood flowed from my face to my sinking heart.

Finally, she hung up the phone, directed me to the elevator, and said he was waiting for me.

Shit. This is it. It was the moment I'd waited days for.

Inhaling a deep breath, I walked over to the metallic door and pressed the button. I stepped in once the door slid open and caught a glimpse of my reflection in the steely surface. I hadn't done laundry since I'd arrived home, so the only thing I had to wear was a long black sleeveless maxi dress. I'd paired it with black sneakers and a light jean jacket. My hair was up in its usual messy bun, and I had no makeup on. To be honest, I looked like shit. Maybe it would make my confession more authentic.

My body tensed as the elevator door slid open. My mind snapped back to the present. I took a breath, staring at the man in front of me, just a few feet away. I failed to form any coherent sentence and stepped out, and the door slid closed behind me. *Too late for an escape now.*

"Hi," I muttered, hugging myself, not meeting his gaze.

His lips formed a straight line. His hands were in his jeans pockets, which hung low on his hips, and yeah . . . he wasn't wearing a shirt. *Big fucking surprise.*

"What're you doing here, Julia?" he asked.

The question stung. He had to have an inkling of an idea, or maybe he was just punishing me. I deserved it. "I wanted to talk."

He turned on his heel and started for the mudroom leading into his penthouse. "About?"

I followed him. We passed through the wide hallway and

ambled into the kitchen. "I wanted to apologize and pay for any incurred costs."

He leaned on the kitchen island, supporting himself on his forearms, causing the lines of his chest muscles to pop even more. "What're you talking about?" His brow furrowed.

I crossed my arms. "The contract."

"Is that why you're here?" The volume of his voice rose as he straightened and stepped toward me.

His sudden movement caused me to falter backward. "Yes. No." God, why was I at a loss for words? I bit my lip and looked away from him. "I'm here because I saw your Miami concert."

His head canted. "And?"

"The song."

"Which song?"

Dammit, he knew which fucking song I was talking about. I released a breath. "The last one, 'Sunshine and Madness.'"

He leaned a hip against the edge of the kitchen island. "What about it?"

I already knew the answer to the question, but I had to be sure. "Is it about us?"

A glint of a smile formed on his gorgeous face. "What do you think?"

Stop lollygagging around the subject and fucking say it.

With a slow inhale, I gazed into his russet eyes. "I'm sorry it took me so long to realize this—" My heart and my head were playing tug-of-war with each other. What if he didn't feel the same anymore and was only doing this to get revenge? I was about to make myself *completely* vulnerable to this man.

"What did you realize, Julia?" he prodded.

I released the breath I was holding and glared at him. "Give me a second."

Lucas seemed unfazed by my attitude as he closed the distance between us.

"I know I haven't been completely fair to you. That I let my fears get the best of me." I swallowed. *Just say it.* My pulse raced in my neck. "I love you."

His brow rose, and he stared at the white tiled floor, turning his back to me.

Definitely not the reaction I'd expected.

"Why?"

I frowned. "Why do I love you?"

He nodded.

"Because you make me crazy," I exclaimed. That probably wasn't the most effective way to proclaim my love, but it wasn't far from the truth. My voice cracked as I said, "Every time I'm around you, I can't help but *feel* everything. Ever since my mom left, I've just been going through the motions of life with no passion. Then you came along, and it was like you awakened this fucking . . . creature in me."

He faced me, the corner of his mouth rising. "Are you saying I made you into a zombie?"

I rolled my eyes. "No, stupid." Maybe I was the stupid one. "The opposite."

"You have a lot of nerve showing up like this." His face was void of emotion as he crossed his arms.

This was a dumb idea. "I know."

With anger in his voice, he asked, "How do you know I haven't moved on?"

A lump was forming in my throat, but I didn't let it rise. "I don't know." *Fuck me.* I felt the buildup of tears in my eyes as I prepared for him to tear what was left of my heart to pieces. "I guess . . . I just needed to get that off my chest."

After a few silent moments, he stepped close, grabbed me by the waist, and pulled me against him. He cupped my nape with his free hand, the pad of his thumb brushed my warm cheek, and his dark russet eyes captured mine. "Say it again."

He looked at me so tenderly, with passion and desire that were mine and mine alone. How could I have doubted his feelings for me? How could I have been so fucking blind?

I wrapped my arms around his neck. "I love you, Lucas Verduce."

My lips met his, innocent and tender, until he deepened the kiss and pulled me harder against him. I knew he wasn't the gentle type. It was one of the things I fucking loved. His hand roamed to one of my ass cheeks and squeezed. I let out a squeal, and he smiled against my lips, then pushed his tongue into my mouth.

I didn't realize he'd inched us closer to the couch in the living room until he sat down and I was straddling his lap. He bunched my dress up to my thighs, roaming the silky skin there as he continued to work his mouth on mine. His dick pulsed through his jeans against my already-wet pussy. I'd been wet since I stepped off the elevator. My body knew what it wanted; it had just taken my brain a little longer to realize that.

His lips trailed my jawline to the curve of my neck. He sucked and nipped and grazed his teeth against my pulse. I moaned, biting into my bottom lip.

"Does this mean you forgive me?" I panted as he ground his hips against me.

"What do you think, Sunshine?" He had my dress off in the next instant, revealing my black cotton bra and panties. "Fucking hell, you're so sexy, Jules." He unclasped my bra and pulled it off, then took one of my hardened nipples into his mouth. He sucked my stiff peaks as I writhed against him.

My nails dug into his sculpted shoulders. God, it felt so good to be touched by him. I leaned forward, kissing his tattooed collarbone all the up to the sensitive spot behind his ear. He gripped my hips when I gave it a tantalizing lick.

"I need to be in you," he growled.

Without hesitation, I stood and slipped out of my panties as he pulled his jeans down, letting his cock breathe. We were completely naked in front of each other, and I didn't care. I positioned myself over his length, wanting to tease him a little. His dick parted the wet folds of my pussy. I sank onto him inch by throbbing inch.

"Fuck, Sunshine, you're killing me." His head fell back against the couch cushions.

Once I had him to the hilt, I moved my hips in that same gradual motion. He rested his hands on my thighs, letting me take control. He let me ride him for a good minute or two before he flipped me onto my back.

"I can't fucking take it anymore," he said, thrusting his cock into me, hard.

I screamed. He penetrated me raw and deep. I had an IUD, so I didn't think about it for long, wanting to enjoy the feeling of him against me. Inside me. All over me. His lips grazed every inch of me. He pulled out and plunged into me over and over.

I wanted him to lose it. *Fuck* . . . He was hitting that sensitive spot inside me with every thrust. "Right there," I whimpered.

He kept a steady rhythm. "Come all over my fucking cock." He leaned forward and placed his forehead against mine. "Okay?"

"Okay."

He reached between our perspiring bodies and rubbed circles around my clit, sending me over the edge within the next few minutes.

I wasn't quiet about it. The walls of my pussy clenched him hard, and my legs trembled.

"Fuck." His chest vibrated. He chased his release in long languid strokes before his dick throbbed inside me as I came down from my own orgasm. He kissed me long and hard and collapsed on top of me, laying his head above my right breast.

After a few minutes of us catching our breath, Lucas supported himself on his forearms. He stared into my eyes for what seemed like the hundredth time that day and said, "I love you too, Sunshine."

Lucas hadn't told me where we were going; he'd just pulled up in a black limousine in front of my studio and told me to get in. He had that irritating trademark smirk on his face, which still caused my blood to boil.

"Can you at least give me a hint where we're going?" I asked, resting my elbow on the door. He knew I hated surprises. "Are you taking me somewhere to kill me?" I joked.

He raised an eyebrow. "Why would I do that?"

"Because you're tired of me." It came out as more of a statement than a question.

A grin crept onto his handsome features. He'd grown his hair out since retiring from his rock star lifestyle. Honestly, I liked his shaggy hair. It gave me something to hold on to.

"Why are you smiling?" he asked. "You weren't thinking dirty thoughts, were you?"

I bit my lower lip. "About who?"

He kept a smirk on his face as the limo came to a stop. "We're here."

The sidewalk was busy with people coming and going. He gestured to a brick building connected to others of the same style. We climbed out of the limo, and I stared up at it.

"You wanna check out your new studio?"

My eyes snapped to him, wide and disbelieving. "What?" I brought my hand over my mouth, not knowing what else to say. *He bought me a fucking studio?*

He held up a single key and placed it in my other hand. "Come on."

I unlocked the thick glass door and walked inside. It was much bigger than my current studio. With this space, I could take on more students. My business had really taken off after Lucas quit the band. People found out that I'd danced in "My Crimson Love," and the rest was history.

There were mirrors on the back wall with a long iron barre attached. The reception desk was all black and appeared to be brand-new. There was also a little room where the parents could sit and watch their children. My eyes welled up.

"How long have you been planning this?" I asked, facing Lucas.

He had his hands in the pockets of his jeans. "A while." His gaze went to the desk behind me. "What's that?"

I turned and saw a little black box on the reception desk. How had I missed that? Wait. Little black box . . . Was he . . . ?

My breath hitched, and my brow rose. I met Lucas's dark eyes.

"Maybe it's a welcome gift." He shrugged.

My eyes narrowed. He knew damn well it wasn't a welcome gift. I made my way over to the desk with clammy palms, and my heart in my throat. I picked up the velvet box and flipped the lid open. I frowned. There was nothing in it.

"Sunshine," Lucas called, his tone tender with a hint of nervousness.

I turned slow and steady to find him on one knee, holding a yellow diamond solitaire set in a black band between his thumb and index finger.

"Holy shit," I murmured, and yeah . . . the fucking waterworks were coming.

"Julia Blackwell, you have been the most infuriating, most difficult person I've ever met, but you've been such an inspiration and, despite what you think, a light in my life. I love you. Marry me. Make me the happiest ex–rock star in New York."

I couldn't help but smile through the tears falling down my cheeks. "I'm gonna have to think about that one."

He glared at me, the annoyance apparent on his handsome face.

"Yes!" I threw my arms around him and pressed my lips to his. He placed the ring on my finger. "Wow, it fits."

"What did you expect?" He straightened, his hands resting on my hips.

I looked at him. "Does this mean I get half of that new record label you're starting?"

"Sunshine, you can have it all if you want." He kissed my forehead, slow and fervent.

I rested my head against his chest, listening to the beat of his heart. "No. I just want you."

He squeezed me a little tighter against him. "I'm glad we finally agree on something."

*If you enjoyed this book, please leave a review.
It'll help the author out more than you know!*

THE MAD LOVE SERIES

Sweetness
AND
MADNESS

ALYSSA GREEN

LIFE'S UNYIELDING MARCH FORWARD TAUGHT ME ITS hardest lesson: it waits for no one. After my mother's death, I stepped away from the ballet company and assisted my best friend, Julia, in launching her dance studio. I was grateful for the opportunity but couldn't shake the feeling of being adrift, unsure of my true calling. So, I resigned.

Lucas Verduce, Julia's husband, had offered me a job at his flourishing record label. My role was mostly behind-the-scenes, but the thrill of being part of something new, something pulsating with potential, was exciting. And it brought me into the orbit of Ethan Miller—a man whose charisma was as unsettling as it was captivating. Over the last year, a strange sort of friendship had formed between us.

My commitment to LV Productions had been unwavering. My boss could make an exception, after all. It wasn't as though I'd ever missed a day. *What am I supposed to do with these?* I stared at them for a moment, then remembered I was supposed to distribute them among the parties involved, including Lucas. He still liked keeping physical copies of contracts.

Despite the calming scent of eucalyptus wafting from the diffuser, the office air was heavy with a sense of routine and unspoken expectations. The ticking clock was a constant reminder of the doctor's appointment looming over me. I had an hour left but so much to finish.

I smoothed out my oversize beige waffle sweater and tucked a strand of wavy dark hair behind my ear before picking up the copies from the printer tray.

"Mia."

My gaze trailed up the length of Ethan's sexy frame. From his perfectly tailored black trousers to his royal-blue button-down, this man teetered on the precipice of being a professional and a tease.

Goddammit.

His sleeves were rolled up to his elbows, revealing toned sun-kissed forearms.

I blinked out of my trance. "Hey."

He stopped a few feet from me, close enough that his citrusy bergamot scent filled my nose. "Are you busy?"

This is torture. Absolute fucking torture. Sometimes I questioned my sanity in accepting this job. "Nope, just making copies for that new solo artist you found."

"Sounds exciting. I actually wanted to talk to you about something," he said.

"Oh?" I waited for him to go on.

"It's more of a personal favor," he said.

With an eye roll, I prodded, "Well, spit it out already."

A corner of his mouth tilted up. "My parents hold Thanksgiving dinner at their house every year. And every year, without fail, they try to set me up with someone. I was thinking I could stay ahead of the game and actually bring someone for a change."

I'd met Ethan's family at Lucas and Julia's wedding at the beginning of the year. His mom, dad, sister, and niece seemed to like me well enough. But they knew Ethan and I were just friends.

I cocked a brow and grinned. "What does that have to do with me?"

His lips formed a straight line. "Do I have to spell it out?"

I crossed my arms. "Well, if you're gonna give me attitude, yeah."

He let out a dramatic sigh; luckily, I was immune to his theatrics. "Will you be my date? I really don't want them hassling me about settling down . . . again."

Ethan, like everyone else in this industry, seemed to have an aversion to commitment. In the short time I'd known him, I'd learned he didn't talk about settling down. I wasn't any better. I let out a short breath, reminded of my own reluctance to fall in love ever since Kyle's betrayal. We hadn't been official, but it still hurt like we were.

Julia and I had caught Kyle butt-ass naked, fucking some groupie in the back of one of the tour buses. It had been a painful lesson. My trust in relationships had crumbled, and I'd vowed never to let my heart be crushed like that again.

The wounds had left me wary of diving into anything resembling commitment.

Ethan jutted out his bottom lip, making a pouty face. Taking my hand, he squeezed. "Please? I'll pick up 50 percent of your workload for the next week."

"Make it a month and we have a deal."

He smirked. "You drive a hard bargain, Mia Cruz. But you have a deal."

I pulled my hand away to check my watch. "Shit, I have to go." I gave him the copies of the contract I'd been holding.

He took them. "Where? Do you need a ride?"

I smiled, my boot heels clicking against the tile floor as I made my way toward the exit. "Nope. Why don't you get started on some of my tasks? I'll text you the list."

I ARRIVED AT THE SPECIALIST'S OFFICE IN TIME TO FILL out all the paperwork with the receptionist. This was my second visit in a month. *It's probably nothing.* Just stress from starting a new job. After the No Blood, No Alibi tour last year, thinking it was period cramps, I let it go. Recently, the pain had started to become unbearable. Dr. Colton wanted to meet with me in person. In my experience, they usually called with the results.

I sat in front of his modern black desk, unable to speak. My breaths came out shallow, and lightheadedness swept over me. The word caught in my throat as I sat there in the sterile white office. He'd said the words no one ever wants to hear: *you have cancer.*

The oncologist, Dr. Colton, jotted something down on his tablet, a strand of blond hair falling out of place onto his forehead. "Your treatment plan will begin with surgical intervention, specifically a unilateral oophorectomy. This procedure will involve the removal of one fallopian tube and ovary. After, we'll initiate adjuvant chemotherapy, utilizing a combination of cytotoxic agents tailored to your specific diagnosis."

My head dipped, eyes wide as they flickered between the doctor and the floor.

He stood and began picking brochures off the far wall. "The surgery will be followed by a series of chemotherapy cycles. We'll closely monitor your progress through regular blood tests, imaging studies, and tumor-marker assessments."

Taking the pamphlets from him, I tried to focus on the details, but they blurred in front of my eyes. I blinked back tears, refusing to let them fall in front of him. "Will I be able to have kids?"

"You should still be able to conceive, but unfortunately, it will be more difficult. The chances we'll have to perform a hysterectomy later in life are high," he said. "We're aiming for maximum efficacy with minimal invasiveness. You're in the early stages, which significantly improves your prognosis."

I cleared my throat, my gaze meeting his once more. "Thank you, Doctor."

"We'll try to get you scheduled after Thanksgiving," he said. "You can get through this, Mia. The best thing to do right now is to live your life as normally as possible."

Normal? All I could do was nod.

We discussed what would come next, but my mind was swirling, unable to focus on what he was saying. Before I knew it, I was stepping outside into the chilly New York air. I looked up at the baby-blue sky, overwhelmed by the enormity of it all. With three words, my life as I knew it had shattered.

THE SILENCE OF MY APARTMENT ECHOED THE VOID gnawing at my heart. *This really sucks.* I sat on my couch staring at the information packet the doctor had given me.

Surgery. Chemotherapy. Radiation.

I read about the type of cancer I had. Tears welled up in my eyes, brimming at the edges before cascading down my cheeks. They fell onto the paper, each droplet landing with a soft tap.

How can I possibly live life normally?

I didn't have family in the States. My father moved back to the Philippines before Thanksgiving last year, but I supposed I'd have to tell him the shitty news. With Mom having passed from cancer, this would hit him hard.

I should tell him, but maybe I could wait a bit. If the doctor could get rid of it as easily as he spoke about it, maybe there was no point in telling anyone. He had the right to know. *He's my father.* But right now, I could only take care of myself.

My cell vibrated. Glancing at the screen, I answered the call and did my best to sound normal. "Hey, babe."

"Are we still on for lunch?" Julia's sweet-yet-sometimes-brash voice echoed through the speaker, a quality that made her the perfect ballet teacher.

"I'm gonna need a rain check, Jules," I said, sinking deeper into the cushions. God, I was tired. I'd popped a painkiller before sitting down, and it was starting to kick in. Fast.

"Are you sleeping already?" she asked.

"No. I just got in."

She didn't say anything for a second. "How's work?"

I tried my best not to sound annoyed. "Can we talk about all of this later?" I grabbed the remote from the coffee table in front of me and turned on Netflix.

"Fine." Julia sighed. "When was the last time you were properly fucked?"

Damn, how long has it been? I'd been too wrapped up in the job transition and my stomach cramps to notice. It had probably been a few months at the most.

"Fuck . . . That long?"

I repeated something she'd said to me before she'd started dating Lucas. "I don't count anyone who can't make me come."

She giggled. "I guess we'll have to find you someone who can, then maybe you'll stop being bitchy."

I hadn't been myself these past weeks, but that was due to the pain I was in. However, I couldn't help but laugh at her stupid remark. It was one of the many things I could count on from her.

A few seconds later, lightheadedness swept through me. "Look, I gotta go, but I'll text you later."

With a groan, she said, "Just tell me you don't wanna talk to me."

"You're being unnecessarily difficult today," I mused.

"Fine, but you better text me."

"Don't you have a husband to annoy now?" I teased.

"Text me," was her final warning before we exchanged goodbyes and hung up.

I tossed my cell onto the cushion next to me. How had everything changed so quickly? Just yesterday, my biggest worry was work, but now it was death. That word alone sent chills down my spine. It felt like I was in a bubble, watching the world move on while I was stuck here, frozen in fear. Julia would try to be there for me in her own way, but she couldn't truly understand. The thought of attending Ethan's family's Thanksgiving dinner lingered in my mind. It was only about four weeks away.

God, I'm exhausted.

<u>**The Akrani Gods series**</u>

Book I: Of Flesh and Steel

Book II: Of Blood and Onyx

Book III: Of Wrath and Chaos (*coming soon!*)

<u>**The Mad Love series**</u>

Book II: Sweetness and Madness

Book III: Passion and Madness (*coming soon!*)

<u>**Standalones**</u>

Half Blood: The Tale of Samara

Saints and Sinners (*coming soon!*)

Acknowledgments

I would like to thank my lovely critique partners for helping me put together my first of many, rock star romance stories. When I first started this project, it was a mess. Thank you Lana, Kasey, and Brittany!

A huge thank you to Natalia Leigh at Enchanted Ink Publishing for accepting another hefty project from me. Your edits just make my stories more concise every time.

To my beta readers: Thank you to Rachel, and Veronica for leaving me honest and helpful feedback. It really helped to tighten the story.

As usual, I'd like to thank my husband, Bobby, who has been a huge support in helping me follow this dream. To all my close family and friends for their continued support. You all rock!

Alyssa Green

Alyssa is a US Navy veteran with a degree in psychology. She's a multifaceted person who enjoys a variety of activities. When she's not writing or reading, she can be found editing for clients, traveling the United States with her husband and dog, Fiona, or hiking and exploring the outdoors. She's also a lifelong learner who has been taking classes through the Editorial Freelancers Association to improve her skills as a freelance editor.

WWW.AUTHORALYSSAGREEN.COM

facebook.com/authoralyssagreen

instagram.com/author_alyssa_green

tiktok.com/@authoralyssagreen

amazon.com/author/alyssagreen